DEAR BLUE SKY

MARY SULLIVAN

Nancy Paulsen Books

An Imprint of Penguin Group (USA) Inc.

NANCY PAULSEN BOOKS
A division of Penguin Young Readers Group.
Published by The Penguin Group.
Penguin Group (USA) Inc., 375 Hudson Street, New York, NY 10014, U.S.A.
Penguin Group (Canada), 90 Eglinton Avenue East, Suite 700, Toronto, Ontario M4P 2Y3,
Canada (a division of Pearson Penguin Canada Inc.).
Penguin Books Ltd, 80 Strand, London WC2R 0RL, England.
Penguin Ireland, 25 St. Stephen's Green, Dublin 2, Ireland
(a division of Penguin Books Ltd).
Penguin Group (Australia), 250 Camberwell Road, Camberwell, Victoria 3124, Australia
(a division of Pearson Australia Group Pty Ltd).
Penguin Books India Pvt Ltd, 11 Community Centre, Panchsheel Park, New Delhi—110 017, India.
Penguin Group (NZ), 67 Apollo Drive, Rosedale, Auckland 0632, New Zealand
(a division of Pearson New Zealand Ltd).
Penguin Books (South Africa) (Pty) Ltd, 24 Sturdee Avenue, Rosebank,
Johannesburg 2196, South Africa.
Penguin Books Ltd, Registered Offices: 80 Strand, London WC2R 0RL, England.

Published simultaneously in Canada.
Printed in the United States of America.
Design by Marikka Tamura.
Text set in Fournier MT Std.
Library of Congress Cataloging-in-Publication Data
Sullivan, Mary, 1966–
Dear Blue Sky / Mary Sullivan. p. cm.
Summary: "Shortly after Cass's big brother is deployed to fight in Iraq, Cass becomes pen pals
with an Iraqi girl who opens up her eyes to the effects of war"—Provided by publisher.
[1. Brothers and sisters—Fiction. 2. Iraq War, 2003—Fiction. 3. War—Fiction. 4. Pen pals—Fiction.
5. Down syndrome—Fiction. 6. Family life—Fiction.] I. Title.
PZ7.S95315De 2012 [Fic]—dc23 2011046952
ISBN 978-0-399-25684-4
1 3 5 7 9 10 8 6 4 2

For my mother and father

CONTENTS

CHAPTER 1

PEAZE TRAIN

IN THE DREAM it was dark and Sef called me in a whisper. "Cass. Come on, Cass." My brother was standing in the doorway of my room, like he used to when he'd wake me to go running. I threw back my covers and touched my feet to the ground. Right when I stood, he blew up into about a million pieces. There wasn't a sound. Each piece of him was like a snowflake falling, slowly cutting through the air. It was strangely beautiful.

When I woke, I knew one thing: Sef couldn't go to war.

On the Saturday before Sef was supposed to go to Iraq, Dad stood outside our house smiling at the giant flag that flapped like a sail over the sky in front of the brick apartment building at the end of our street. Whenever Dad gave directions, he'd say, "Then turn left onto Hawthorne. You'll see an American flag straight ahead. You can't miss it. It's got to be the biggest flag ever made. We're the tan house on the left." If it weren't for that flag, our street would have been just like every other street in Hillview. The middle of nowhere.

Hillview, otherwise known as Hellview, had cornfields, tobacco farms, apple orchards, Swallow River, Layla's Pizza, Fresh Café, and a state hospital on top of the hill where we went sledding every winter. Dad would tell Mom sometimes, "If you don't watch out, that's where you'll end up." She'd say, "I'll be visiting you."

Anyway, Dad must have forgotten about daylight savings when he said that about the flag. It was early November, and the sky was charcoal gray by the time people started arriving for Sef's going-away party. You couldn't see anything, just the lights in the houses around us. Everyone in our neighborhood was invited, even the Klinmans, who had a WAR IS NOT THE ANSWER sign staked in their front yard. Mom was against the war too, though she wouldn't say so in front of Dad and Sef.

Upstairs, my sister, Van, was putting on eyeliner in the bathroom. Her long dark hair hung down her back. I was the only one in our family with light hair and pale skin. "It must be some long-lost relative on my side," Mom said. She was Irish, and Dad was Italian. I didn't care. I just pulled my hair back in a ponytail anyway.

Van was so pretty, I couldn't stand to look at her. And she always did everything right. She dabbed her eyelashes with a wad of toilet paper.

I asked her, "What if he doesn't come back?"

"Sef?"

"Of course Sef. Who else?"

"He has to come back," she said matter-of-factly.

"Why? Why does he have to?"

"Because if he didn't come back—" Van stopped, glancing up.

Mom was standing behind me in a blue cashmere dress and stockings. We waited now to see if she had heard what we were talking about.

"What? Did I miss something?" She turned to me and asked, "Are you wearing *that*?"

I had on the same thing I always did, black jeans, a T-shirt, and Converse sneakers. I wasn't into dressing up, and I was never going to be a beauty queen, especially not with a scar like a crescent moon on the side of my eye from when I ran through a glass door. Not that I *wanted* to be a beauty queen. I didn't. When she was eighteen, Mom was Miss New Hampshire. She was beautiful, like Van.

I said to Mom now, "Do you think Sef really cares what I'm wearing?"

For a second, she looked like she was about to cry, just like she did that night Sef told us he'd joined. He said it like he was just telling us he'd gone to the movies.

"No, you can't do that to me," Mom had said that night. "Troops are dying there. They're coming home in body bags."

The war had been going on for two years.

Sef had stared at his lasagna. "I have to. Besides, Dad said I could go if I wanted. He did it. His father did too. I'm just carrying on the family tradition." He smiled a little.

"What about college?" Mom's voice rose. "I thought you were taking a year off and then you were going to college, like your friends?"

"That was your idea, not mine."

"Tell me you're joking, honey." She smiled at him. "You're not really doing this, are you?"

"I don't like body bags. No body bags," Jack groaned. He rolled his head back and forth.

A choking sound came out of Mom's mouth. "No, baby," she said to Jack. "Don't even say it, because he's not going."

Though he was eight, Jack was the baby. He was small and waddled when he walked, and he wore thick glasses. He was "special," Mom liked to say with a smile. "Just a little slow, that's all." He was her Down syndrome baby.

To me he was just Jack. Sef was the favorite, and Van and I were in between.

"Say something, Joe." Mom turned to Dad. "Please."

The only noise around the table was Dad's fork scraping his plate. He didn't look up. He finished chewing and then said, "He's old enough to decide what he wants to do with his life."

"With his life?" Mom repeated. "With his *life?*"

Sef tapped his fingers on the table and looked out the window over the sink.

"I don't want you to go, Sef," Mom said.

"Me either," I said. For once I agreed with Mom.

In the dark on the porch, I could hear the flag slapping against itself. The smoke rose in thin streams from the grill, drifting in between Sef and his friends, who were sitting on coolers of drinks. Jason pushed his long red hair back. "Isn't it, like, two hundred degrees in Iraq?"

"I think about three hundred," Sef said.

"Whatever it is, it's good I'm not going. I wouldn't last a day."

"I hope I do," Sef said.

4

"Don't even say it, man. In fourteen months, we're going to be sitting here again, and I'll personally kick your ass if you're not," Greg said. The biggest of them, he played football at UMass.

Dad poked the charcoal and popped a cannoli in his mouth. Inside, people were arriving. We could hear the bell, then the *click click* of Mom's high heels each time she swung open the door and said hello in her party voice.

I was standing by the porch door, watching and waiting.

Sef glanced up at me. "Hey, Cass."

When Sef smiled, lines appeared around his mouth and eyes that I hadn't noticed before. He was bigger since training, or harder or something. His long hair and baby face were gone.

"Hey," I said.

"You're going to keep running, aren't you?" he asked me.

"Yeah." Sef and I had been running in the morning for the last two years. When I ran with him, nothing else mattered. The whole world was ours. Sef tried to get me to join the track team, but I liked running to run, and because it was with him. I reached into the cooler and pulled out an orange soda. I said, "I'll keep running if Dad goes with me."

"I'd like to see that," Sef said.

"What?" Dad said. He slapped his thigh. He was wearing his plaid shorts, even though there was a cool breeze. "You think I can't run?"

"Ever seen Homer Simpson run?" Jason asked.

Dad sucked in his stomach and stirred the charcoal, the smoke rising, disappearing in the night.

They laughed and tossed their empty soda cans. I was going

to miss this—having all of them around like this. But things had already changed when Sef's friends left for college. Sef was the only one to stay in Hillview.

Van's boyfriend, Finn, came to the porch door with his guitar. He was a junior, and his band, Solar Train, had won second prize at the high school talent show. Van had never had a boyfriend until this year. Now she had Finn, and she was freshman Homecoming Queen. Mom was thrilled, but Van seemed anxious all the time now, like someone was going to see her doing something wrong.

"It's Finn," I told the others.

"All right, our live entertainment's here. How about a little Sinatra, Finny?" Dad sang out, "I get a kick out of you. I get a kick every time I see you standing there—"

Jason and Greg started cracking up.

Finn frowned and brushed his curly brown hair back from his face. "Is he joking?" he asked.

"I don't think so. He's Italian, remember?" Mom laughed.

"I don't know any Sinatra," Finn said.

"Go on out there and sing something." Mom gave him a little push.

Finn's hand lifted nervously in a half wave as he stepped out onto the porch. He ducked when everyone clapped and hooted. Someone placed a chair in the middle of the porch, and Finn sat down and started tuning his guitar. On his case was a sticker that said MAKE MUSIC NOT WAR.

Van watched from the other side of the screen door. She was a vegetarian, and the smell of burgers, steaks, and hot dogs made her sick.

"You taking requests?" Jason asked.

"How about the Dropkick Murphys?" Greg asked.

"Those punks?" Finn said.

"What?" Greg's smile disappeared. He turned to Sef. "What punks?"

A branch snapped, and I saw Jack crouched down behind the back of the porch in his camouflage pants and shirt. For days he'd been telling everyone that he was going to war with Sef. Jack was one of the boys, and as Dad said, all the boys were for the war. Jack had been hiding since the party started. His dark hair stuck out of the sides of his Red Sox cap, and his almond eyes were focused on Finn. He had such an intensity when he locked his eyes on you, like he could see right through you.

Finn played a few chords to a round of applause. Then he lowered his head and sang, "I've been happy lately, thinking about good things to come."

Sef stared disbelieving at Finn, who kept on singing.

"Out on the edge of darkness there rides a peace train—"

"What is this crap? Are you kidding me?" Greg said, standing, throwing his arms back.

"'Peace Train'? What is this, poetry hour?" Sef asked.

Dad just shook his head and disappeared behind the smoke of the grill as he set the steaks sizzling. Jack's eyes darted around the porch, finally narrowing on Finn. I knew that look. Jack picked up an aluminum bat someone had left on the porch steps. I should have stopped him then, but I thought if he did something really bad, then Sef would have to stay.

Jack bolted up the porch stairs with the bat raised over his head, running straight for Finn.

"Whoa, Jack!" Sef stepped in front of Jack.

Finn stopped playing and opened his eyes in time to see Sef grab the bat from Jack.

Sef twisted the bat up over his head. "Hey, what are you doing, buddy? The music's pretty lame, but not enough to kill him."

"Give it to me! It's mine, and I'm going with you!" Jack tried to wrestle the bat back.

Sef tossed the bat and did "the Jack." That's what we called it when we had to get behind Jack and wrap our arms tight around him until he stopped going crazy. Jack was so transparent. I wished I could be more like that, instead of holding everything in. All week I'd been keeping everything inside—Sef leaving, my friend Sonia not talking to me, and Mom walking around with a weird glazed look in her eyes. I wanted to run, swinging a bat and yelling at Sef not to go to Iraq.

Finn backed past me, through the screen door. "Whoa, dude. He's got some totally uncool karma."

Greg and Jason threw their heads back and laughed so hard, Jason tripped over a cooler.

Jack kept howling. "I'm going with you tomorrow! I'm going!"

"Hey, take it easy." Sef kept Jack's arms pinned. "And anyway, you don't want to go, I'm telling you."

"I do! You're going," Jack screamed. "And I'm going with you—I'm going! Going—"

Sef stood Jack on the cooler so they were eye level. "Listen, buddy, I need you to stay here and take care of Mom and everyone else while Dad's at work. You're the one to do it."

Jack frowned, tears and smudged dirt running down his face. "No. Nooo!"

"You're the next guy in line. You have to stay." Sef let his arms fall. "Besides, you'd miss Christmas."

Jack froze. "Christmas presents."

"No presents in Iraq. It's too far to mail anything. Nothing big anyway, maybe a few chocolate bars, that's it. Listen, I'll be back before you know it, I promise."

Sef's friends circled Jack, slapping him on the back and laughing. "Hey, we need you here, too," they said.

"We really need you, man," Greg said. "Looks like you scared Finn away."

"Hopefully he's taking a ride outta here on his *peace train*," Jason said.

"Peaze train," Jack said.

Greg put Jack up on his shoulders and marched him around the porch. "This is a peaze train."

They passed Jack around with his arms extended like he was Superman. They hollered and whooped it up, and Jack went around and around the porch until the steaks and dogs were cooked. Then we all went inside to eat, everyone but Sef. "Come on, you have to eat," they said. "Better eat while you can, before you get those ready-packs."

"I'll be right in," he said. "I just need a minute."

I could just see his outline in the dark, his arm rising and falling with each swig from his drink. Music was playing inside, so it was impossible to hear if the flag was flapping the way it did, but I wondered if he was listening for it. That *slap flap, slap flap.* I watched him through the door. I didn't take my eyes off him because I was afraid if I did, he'd disappear. I was running out of time.

CHAPTER 2

LOST

DAD LIFTED HIS glass to make a toast. "When Sef first told us he joined the marines, I said to myself, *Of course he did*. He's doing it for our country, just like I did and my father did and his father did. He's going over there to get the job done. It's in our blood. But my son—he's worth a million—"

"No Christmas presents!" Jack shouted.

Some people laughed.

Dad looked around the room. "That's right, no Christmas presents. I couldn't have said it better myself. They don't know how lucky they are, getting my boy to fight for their country. To Sef. God bless him."

The room exploded into cheers and hollers, and people threw their glasses back. Sef just smiled like he was embarrassed and didn't quite know what he was doing in the middle of all of this.

Mrs. Vasaturo from across the street came up to Sef. "You be careful over there, Sef, honey. And come back to us real soon."

Other neighbors and friends lined up to put their arms around

Sef, shake his hand, and give their last good wishes. Some of the women held on too long. In the summer when he took his shirt off to mow the lawn, Mrs. Fischer next door would come out to garden and Mrs. Henderson would walk her pug up and down our street.

Mom marched out, holding the cake high. It was a sheet cake of the flag with the words "OD BLESS YOU, SEF! We love you!" written in blue cursive. The *G* had gotten scraped or eaten off by Jack. Mom started cutting pieces and passing them around. She kept her party smile on, and everyone smiled back at her and told her how strong she was.

There were so many people around Sef that I couldn't even see him. I followed Van to the kitchen, where she turned and went out through the open mudroom door that led to the garage.

Finn was sitting on the stool at Dad's workspace, playing guitar. Our next-door neighbor Kristen Adams was standing too close to him, nodding her head, letting her hair swish side to side. Her tiny T-shirt showed off the gold loop through her belly button. She was in eighth grade, between Van and me.

"What are you guys doing?" Van asked.

Finn turned, paused for a second, and then kept right on singing, "Try to live again, the first cut—"

Kristen looked from Finn to Van to me as the song ended. "That was, like, so cool, Finn. Thanks. I guess I'll go back to the party."

Van looked like she was going to cry.

Finn bent over his guitar and said, "What? I didn't do anything. I'm just playing music."

"The life of a rock star," Van said sarcastically.

"Yeah," Finn said. "Come here."

She did.

I got out of there fast. The night air was getting cold. The bird feeder Sef made for Mom years ago swung from the lowest branch of the sycamore. One of its sides hung askew, and it banged against the tree over and over. I yanked at the rope, pulling hard until it finally loosened and fell to the ground. I stood there for a long time, not knowing if I should leave the bird feeder there or try to fix it. Then I heard someone laughing and went back inside.

Sef and his friends were getting ready to leave.

"Thanks for everything, Dad," Sef said. He hugged Dad and then turned to Mom.

Her shoulders shuddered, and her whole body seemed to become smaller, just for a second. Then she snapped back to her party self.

"I won't be out long. Thanks, Mom."

"This good-bye is easy compared to tomorrow's," Mom said. Just as she stepped forward to kiss him, Jack jumped on Sef's back and wrapped his arms around Sef's neck.

Sef grabbed Jack's hands. "See you in the morning, champ."

Jack wouldn't let go. Dad had to wedge him off.

"Hey, where's Van?" Sef asked.

"Van!" Dad yelled. "Get over here and say good night to your brother."

"I think she got in a fight with Finn," I told them.

"Better her than me." Greg slammed his fist into his palm.

"I'll show him a peace train," Dad said.

"Peaze," Jack said.

Everyone laughed until Van came in. Her eyes were red.

"Bye, Sef."

"See you tomorrow, Van." He pushed up her chin with his fingers. "Do me a favor?"

"Okay."

"Don't let anyone get you down."

She nodded.

"You know I'm not leaving until you smile, right?"

She did. A little. When Van and Finn first started dating, she was so happy. She let me help pick outfits for her to wear, and we listened to CDs of Solar Train that Finn had made. Tonight it seemed like she was playing a game that she couldn't win.

Sef turned to me. "Are you going to be ready tomorrow morning?"

"Sure. Are you?"

He laughed and looked at all of us standing there, waiting for him to leave. "You guys know you're the best, right?"

"Yeah," Jack answered. "I know."

"All right. I'm glad someone around here knows."

He followed his friends out into the dark, and I was sure then that nothing would ever be the same again.

We listened to their car drive away. Dad said, "That went by fast. It was a good party, Gracie."

Mom sank onto the couch. "Now it's over."

"He'll be all right, Grace. He will."

"I never wanted him to go. It was your idea."

"Jack, Cass, go upstairs. Party's over. Get ready for bed," Dad told us.

We stepped over someone's broken wineglass and started

upstairs. When we were almost at the top, we heard Mom say, "If he comes home without arms and legs, I'll never forgive you."

Jack sat down on the last stair and turned to me. "No arms and legs."

"No," I said. "No way. He has arms and legs. Don't listen to them. Mom's crazy. Come on, let's go."

Jack's eyes were wide. He grabbed my hand. "I want to sleep in Sef's room. Please, please, please."

I didn't think Sef would mind. "Go get your sleeping bag."

He pulled my hand harder.

"Did you pee in it?"

He shrugged.

"I'll get mine."

Van was sitting at her computer with her iPod on. Her side of the room was so neat, it was sickening. Sometimes I'd move a photo or some makeup or something out of place just to see how long it'd take her to put it back where it belonged.

"Van," I said, "why weren't Ally and Nora here tonight?"

She shrugged. "I just wanted Finn to be here, if that's all right with you."

"I just thought it was a little weird, since they've been your friends for years and you've known Finn for a couple of weeks or something."

She turned the volume up on her iPod.

I spun the globe on the floor next to my bed, closed my eyes, and landed my finger on the place I was going to end up living. The Pacific Ocean. I'd need a houseboat. I couldn't exactly build a school for Jack on a houseboat. That was Sef's idea. He said that I'd be good at teaching kids like Jack. Right now I didn't think I could do anything right, never mind build a whole school. I carried my sleeping bag to Jack, who was waiting outside Sef's door with White Kitty, who was really grayish brown with dirt.

"Shut the door. Don't let anyone in," he said. "Just Sef."

"No one's trying to knock the door down, don't worry," I said.

I unrolled my sleeping bag beside Sef's bed. In his camouflage clothes, Jack shimmied inside it and shut his eyes.

Sef had spent his whole life in this room. It had the same wallpaper with tiny silver airplanes. On his desk, there were pictures of girls from his class. They were all pretty with different lengths of dark, feathery hair. And there was the picture of him from a road race. Jason had lost a bet and had to run wearing a Speedo and a girl's tank top. Sef was beside him, laughing. He didn't look like a marine. He looked like my brother.

There was a picture of our family from a barbecue last summer. Everyone was smiling except for me. I always looked like a phony when I smiled for pictures, like someone had come along and taped a stupid look on my face, so I didn't smile. Mom, in a white pleated skirt and sleeveless blouse, wore a big smile, showing her teeth. Her hand rested on Sef's shoulder. Sef was holding up the football he and Dad had been passing back and forth. Kneeling in front of Sef, Jack had to turn his head up to look at Sef.

All our heads were tilted toward Sef, I saw then. I wished I could remember now what it was he had said that made us all look at him. I set the photo back down on his desk. I felt lost.

CHAPTER 3

I DIED

I DIDN'T EVEN realize how much Sef held us together until he was gone. He was the only one who could make Van smile. He was Jack's hero and Dad's best buddy. He was the only one Mom listened to when she'd had too much to drink. And me, I was myself with Sef. I laughed the most with him. Sometimes I thought if people at school saw me at home, they'd ask, "Who is that girl?"

Sef was always watching over us. I remember a fall day years ago when Mom took us to the beach. It was windy and warm as we started over the sand toward the water.

Mom realized she'd left her purse in the car. She yelled for Van and Sef, but they were too far ahead. "Watch Jack," she said to me and turned back toward the parking lot.

I stretched out my arms and let the wind whip around me, breathed in the salty, seaweedy smell. The sand was warm between my toes. I picked up an upside-down horseshoe crab shell by its tail and let the sand pour out. When I held it up to show Jack, he was gone. I dropped the crab and ran toward the sea, the waves like thunder in my ears.

"Jack! Jack!" By the water the sand dropped, forming a bank beneath where the waves crashed. I knew Jack had gone over the embankment. In my mind I saw him in the water, trying to lift his head as the sea pulled him away, and I knew it was my fault.

I saw Sef ahead of me, running to the same edge of sandbank. When I got there, Sef was kneeling on the sand where the waves crashed. He laid Jack down and pounded him hard on the back. Jack choked and coughed, spitting up, his arms flapping like he was trying to fly away. It happened to Jack, but it felt like I was drowning. I touched Jack's face. His eyes were white and watery like they were floating far away. My heart was pounding, and I couldn't breathe.

"Don't do that again!" Sef yelled. "Never!"

I didn't know if he was talking to Jack or me.

Van stood back, her pants wet to the tops of her legs. "He could have died," she said.

"I died," Jack said.

"No, Jack, you didn't," Sef said.

"There's Mom," Van said.

Her black purse banged against her side, and her long sweater flew out behind her. She cried when she saw us. She fell into the sand on her knees and took Jack and rocked him back and forth for a long time.

"I'm sorry, Mom," I said, and then I took off running down the beach until I collapsed in the sand. Until I could breathe again. After a while, Sef came for me. His clothes were still wet. He handed me a smooth gray-blue skipping stone that fit in the palm of my hand. I never threw it. I kept it in my pocket.

"Come on, Cass," he said. "It's okay. Jack's okay. He found a horseshoe crab. Come on. I'll race you." And we ran as fast as we could through the sand. It felt so good to breathe hard, to suck air in and to sweat out the fear. I knew what would have happened if Sef hadn't been there. Every morning since then, Sef and I had gone running.

When we got home, Jack held the horseshoe crab up by the tail for Dad. "I died," he said. A tiny trickle of sand fell to the ground.

"Yeah?" Dad popped a napoleon into his mouth. "And then you rose again?"

"And walked across the water," Mom said triumphantly.

Dad poured them drinks. We never talked about it again.

That's how we were—we didn't talk about things.

CHAPTER 4

BRING 'EM ON

I WAS MAD at Sonia for not coming to Sef's party, but the weekend before hadn't gone so well. Her parents had come over to watch the Patriots game. Even though they lived only two blocks away, they drove because of the freak storm that blew snowflakes the size of my hands. Mom watched out the window as the LeClaires backed their Volvo down our driveway. "They're here!" she sang.

Sonia came in first, carrying a tray of beads and shaking the snow from her long blond hair. She looked so pretty and so together.

"Hey," she said to me.

"Hey."

"It's crazy out there."

"I know," I said. "Jack's been howling because Mom wouldn't let him outside."

"Only Jack." She laughed and started to spread her beads out on the table. I'd told her I'd help her string some necklaces for her new jewelry business.

Sonia's father, Eric, draped his arm over Sef's shoulders. A lawyer, he was slim and had clean-cut boyish looks and sandy slicked-back hair. "One more week, Sef. Are you ready?"

"As ready as I'll ever be."

"You're going to kick some ass over there."

"That's the plan."

"Bring 'em on!"

Susan shook her head at her husband as she set a platter of nachos on the coffee table. Like Sonia, Susan was Barbie-doll pretty. "You've got to think of something new to say," she said.

"What's he saying now?" Mom asked.

"Nothing," Dad said. "You don't want to know."

Sonia rolled her eyes at me.

"Nice!" Eric shouted. "Killer catch."

Everyone turned to the TV. Dad stayed in his leather chair. Mom sat on the couch between Eric and Susan on one half of the L couch, and on the other was Jack in his Tom Brady shirt and Sef.

"Kick some ass! Bring 'em on!" Jack shouted.

"Jack," Mom asked, "where'd you hear that?"

Jack chanted louder and louder, "Kick some ass! Bring 'em on!" Then he jumped up and pulled down his underwear and sweatpants.

"For God's sake, Jack," Mom said.

Mom pulled Jack's pants up while Eric roared laughing. "Well, that gets the afternoon off with a bang! It's going to be hard for Tom Brady to top this."

"Let's go to your room," Sonia said. She looked disgusted.

Upstairs, Sonia held out the oblong glass beads strung in a two-brown, one-pink pattern. "That was really gross," she said.

"Jack?" I asked. "Jack's not gross. Jack is Jack. You know that."

"You realize your family is pretty weird sometimes, don't you?" she said.

"It's not like your family is perfect," I answered.

"I know," she admitted. "When we were getting ready, Dad told my mom she had to lose weight. For like the billionth time. She freaked out, of course."

"Your mom's not even fat."

"Tell her that," Sonia said. "I don't get how it's okay for men to be fat and not women. My mom was crying."

"Well, I guess it's not okay for men to be fat either, because my mom hides my dad's pastries. But he usually finds them and eats them anyway."

Sonia laughed. Her blue eye shadow sparkled in the light, and her highlighted blond hair fell over her face. "Thanks for helping me. I want to make my own money so Mom can't tell me what I can get when we go shopping. She doesn't like buying me makeup." She glanced up at me. "You'd look amazing in my silver eye shadow. Can I try some on you? Just for fun?"

"No way. I hate makeup."

I could hear Jack outside, yelling at Sef to throw him the ball. I said, "Let's go out and catch snowflakes. We always do that the first time it snows. Remember last year?" We fell over, we were laughing so hard trying to catch the swirling snow in our mouths.

"No, thanks." Sonia's eyes got smaller, and her lip curled up.

I shrugged.

Jack called out, "Touchdown!"

I said, "I can't stop thinking about Sef leaving."

"Everything's always about Sef," she said quietly.

I ignored her. "It's not just that he's the best with Jack, but he always makes everything better."

She knotted her string and cut the ends. "What about Van? She helps, doesn't she?"

"Yeah, but she's always with Finn now."

"That's good, right?"

I shrugged. "I don't know. She doesn't even talk to her old friends anymore. She just doesn't seem like herself."

"Who does she seem like?"

"Someone else. Have you seen her lately? She's obsessed with her clothes and hair and stuff."

"Well, you're not exactly a fashion judge. I mean, I'd die for your hair, and you don't even care what it looks like."

"I do so. A little."

Sonia smiled.

"Anyway, it's weird how she changed so fast." I said it about Van, but I realized I was afraid that Sonia was changing too fast too. I'd seen her list of friends "to get to know better"—as if the friends she had weren't enough anymore. Most of the girls were cheerleaders, like Lisa and Meg, and I didn't really have anything to say to them.

Downstairs, Sef yelled out, "Sweet!" Then we heard, "Flag! What the—?" They cheered and booed and yelled some more.

"I'm almost done with this one," I said, holding up a necklace. "I'll go check the score."

"I'll go too. I'm hungry," Sonia said.

We started down the stairs, carpeted in plush blue after Jack started crawling. We could see Eric in the kitchen fixing a drink beside the sink. Mom walked up to him and reached for the drink. "That for me?"

"You forgot to say please." Eric raised the drink above his head.

She stood on the tips of her toes. One hand pressed against his chest. "Pretty please with a cherry on top?"

Eric smiled with his mouth open. "Are you begging?"

"Oh, my God," Sonia said.

On the other side of Eric, Jack stopped pouring Life cereal into a bowl and looked at them. Mom smiled back at him, then brushed by them both, and skipped out. She didn't see us.

"What was that?" Sonia hissed.

"I don't know."

"Why'd your mom act like that?"

I didn't know what to say. Jack was right there. Sonia's face was red. My stomach turned, and I held on to the banister.

"It's nothing," I said. "My mom's been a little crazy lately with Sef leaving."

"Crazy?" Sonia repeated. "That's a good excuse."

Sonia marched down the rest of the stairs and didn't even look back. I heard her announce, "I don't feel good. I want to go home."

"Oh, honey, what is it? You look flushed. Are you hot?" her mother asked.

"I don't know."

"Why don't I take you home."

"I want Dad to come too," Sonia said.

"Can we wait until the end of the quarter?" Eric asked.

"No." Sonia turned and walked out the front door.

The LeClaires went home, and the Patriots lost.

When I told Sef about it, he said, "That's just Mom. She was probably fooling around, you know how she is."

"You sure about that?" I asked.

"I'll ask her."

"No."

"Yes."

"No."

Sef sighed. "She is having a pretty hard week, Cass."

She wasn't the only one having a hard week. I emailed Sonia, texted, and called, but she didn't answer. She kept her head down and answered with one word when I asked her anything. Then nothing. Zilch. When I carried my tray to our table, she got up and moved to the other end. I sat down where I always did, but no one talked to me. They smiled a little and looked at each other, and I knew they were thinking, *We know. We know about your family. We know there is something wrong with you.* I glanced around the table. Every one of the girls there was closer to Sonia than to me.

There were only two people I really counted on—Sonia and Sef. Sonia wouldn't talk to me, and Sef was leaving for Iraq.

SWALLOW RIVER

WHEN I WOKE Sunday morning, it was dark, but I could see the outline of trees through the window, and I could hear the birds singing. As if today was like any other day.

At nine, they would take Sef to some stupid parking lot where all the families met for the last good-bye. Then buses would take the recruits to the airport. Mom had decided it would be better for her and Dad to go alone with Sef. We were to say our last good-bye at home. No matter what, I wasn't going to cry.

I heard Sef outside our bedroom door. "Cass! Come on, Cassie."

I slid out of bed and put on my sneakers. "Ready," I said, and followed him out the door into the cold morning air.

"You okay?" he asked.

"Yeah, but I didn't sleep much."

"Me either."

We didn't talk much after that. It was enough to concentrate on breathing in and out, putting one foot in front of the other.

We took our usual route down Hawthorne, past the Adamses', the scrubby blackberry bushes, the Hendersons' broken-down Volkswagens, over the long stretch of cornfields, through the woods, and around Turtle Pond. We were going faster than usual, and by the time we were halfway around the pond, sweat was dripping down my face. This was how I always saw my-self—running fast with Sef. What was I going to do tomorrow?

A dog barked across the water, and a duck skimmed over its glassy top, where the sun was slowly spreading its yellow light.

"Aren't they supposed to be leaving?" Sef asked, sucking in his breath.

"Yeah, seems like they stay longer and longer each year."

"Hey, go south, before your asses freeze to the pond!" Sef yelled out, waving his arms.

Back on the road, I caught up to Sef. A couple of early morning cars beeped as they drove by. After today, they wouldn't see us.

"I'm dying," Sef said, slowing to a walk. "You're working me harder than they did at training. Going to Iraq will be easy compared to this."

"Yeah, right."

Sef glanced at me. "Are you going out tomorrow morning? You're not going to quit on me, are you?"

"I don't know."

"You have to, Cass. I'll be back before you know it, so don't get all out of shape on me. Seriously, why don't you get Dad to go with you?"

"Are you kidding? I'd have to hold cannolis in front of him or something."

"That's true. He'd make it to the end of the driveway."

"And Jack would probably whack me over the head with a bat," I said.

Sef laughed and started jogging again. "He came pretty close to nailing Finn. What's up with that guy, anyway? Why was he singing 'Peace Train' when I'm going to Iraq?"

"You mean 'Peaze Train.'"

"Yeah."

"I don't know what Van's thinking. She's been skipping field hockey to go to his band practice."

"Really? He's kind of a flake. She'll get over him. But better keep an eye on her until she does."

"Okay."

"Promise?"

"Yeah."

"Where was Sonia last night?"

I shook my head. "She should have come."

"None of them were there, were they?"

"No. I guess it was because of whatever happened last weekend with Mom and her dad. Sonia's not talking to me."

"I bet it's nothing. Mom was just looped. Think she'll be all right?"

I turned quickly to him. We were supposed to act normal. He had enough to worry about. I tried to smile. "What are you worrying about us for, anyway? We'll be fine."

"I can't believe I'm really going today." He blew out sharp breaths of white air. The sky was pink and blue. "Race you to the driveway."

We took off fast. If I could have stopped time, I would have stopped it then, right before we reached the end of the driveway, with just us running crazy, like no one could ever catch us.

Mom was cooking up eggs and bacon.

"Sef," Jack said. His glasses were crooked. "I need to stay in your room until Christmas. Then I'll go to Iraq with you."

Facing the stove, Mom's shoulders rocked up and down. Her eyes never turned from the frying pan.

"Sure, buddy. My room is all yours," Sef said.

Upstairs, Van was pulling down the lower lids of her eyes to line them with a brown pencil. How could she be bothered today? I got in the shower and let the water pound my back. I had to hold it together at least until Sef left. We were supposed to be normal until then, Mom kept saying, like she knew what normal was. Everything was *until then*.

I didn't want to go downstairs and jumped when Dad yelled, "Cass, get down here. We're taking a family photo. Now!"

He was telling Jack to kneel and Sef to sit down. "It's your chair, Dad," Sef said. "You should sit there."

"Go ahead, Sef. We'll stand around you. That's how your mother wants it."

The perfect family photo, I thought.

"Here. You're here," Mom said to me, pointing to the right of Dad's chair.

I knelt down just like Mom wanted, but no one could make me smile. I sat there, frozen.

"One minute," Dad said, setting the self-timer on his old Canon.

He jumped back and stood behind the right arm of the chair. "Everyone, say spaghetti and meatballs!"

They did. The camera went *click*! They were all smiling. After Dad took our picture, I saw the newspaper tossed on the floor. On the front page, there was a picture of a boy in a uniform like Sef's, smiling up at me. "Springfield Soldier Killed in Baghdad," the caption said. I had to keep telling myself that Sef had chosen to go. He was going because he wanted to go, and he wouldn't let anything bad happen.

It wasn't until it was time to say good-bye that something inside me broke. Something that had been bending since the night Sef said he'd joined the marines. I ran out the front door and kept on running with the wind in my ears. I hurt so much, the only thing I knew to do was run.

I thought if I never said good-bye to Sef, then he wouldn't really be gone. It would be like he was waiting somewhere for me. The thing was, I knew he would understand. I ran in the opposite direction from Turtle Pond, past the apartment building with the giant flag, toward Swallow River and the hollowed-out tree that I liked to sit inside. Even after the freak snowstorm, there were still leaves—rusty brown, light gold, and orange. Where were the bright yellows and reds? They never came this year. Something was the matter with the world.

I stayed there for a long time, staring at the sky, listening to the roar of Swallow River. My chest ached. I traced the curve of my scar. I remembered when I ran into our glass door, cutting open my forehead the day I turned five. It was Sef who held me in the car, pressing cloths to my head. They turned red almost instantly. I asked him, "Did my brain fall out?"

"No. You're going to look really cool. Just wait. You'll be okay. Go faster, Mom, please." He pressed another cloth to my head. "You're good. You're okay."

"It hurts. Is the glass still in there?"

"No. No more glass."

The blood kept gushing out. It covered Sef's hand, arm, and sleeve. It covered the seat underneath me. "Sef, there's too much blood."

"You have lots more, don't worry. You're super brave. Speed it up, Mom."

He held me in the waiting room, pressing packs of gauze on my head, one after another. He held me in the hospital room while I screamed as they sewed fourteen stitches into my skin. He was the one I trusted.

The trees shaded the banks on both sides of the river, and the water shone black and cold. It smelled of mud, cool water, and apples. I would stay until I thought Sef was on the bus with the other marines, heading to the airport.

I closed my eyes and imagined that, when I opened them again, everything would be the same as it was before. Sef would be here, and Sonia would be my best friend. We'd all be driving to Sef's basketball game. The gym would stink of sweat, and we'd clap and sway back and forth in the heat and bright lights, everyone yelling and cheering. We used to go to every game.

Mom was glassy-eyed and slumped on one end of the couch in front of the TV when I got home. Dad and Jack were sitting on the other end. Jack had *The Complete Poems of Emily Dickinson* open on his lap. Mom had a whole shelf of poetry books, though I never saw her reading them anymore.

On the TV, a lady with bobbed blond hair groaned when she saw her son's shirt stained with chocolate milk. The camera cut to her standing in front of the washing machine, spraying the shirt with stain remover. Next thing, she had a clean white shirt. Like magic. She smiled, flashing her shiny teeth.

I didn't call Sonia, I didn't do my homework, I didn't eat supper. I sat on the couch like a zombie, waiting for my life to become clean and white again like the shirt in the commercial.

Later, upstairs, I lay staring into the dark. There was a flash of light by the window. Was it Sef trying to tell me something?

I started looking for signs when Jack was a baby. Little signs that would tell me if he was going to be all right. If he smiled or laughed at me, that was a sign. If there was light in his eyes, that was a sign. Now I was looking for a sign that Sef would be all right.

TINY PIECES

I WOKE IN the same clothes I had on yesterday. I watched the sky turn pale yellow through the window, just making out the shape of the bird feeder that Sef had made for me. It was a wooden box with a triangular roof. There was a neat hole above the perch and slits under the sides of the roof. He gave them to everyone for Christmas presents the year he took shop.

I painted seven blue birds on mine because I was seven that Christmas; most of the paint was washed off by now. After he gave it to me, I asked him, "Why is the hole so small?"

He was resetting the perch on Mom's feeder. He looked up at me. "So the birds can poke their heads in without getting stuck."

"They get stuck in there?"

"Well, they can't get through this small hole, don't worry."

"Would they die in there?"

"No, they won't die."

The white Christmas lights flashed on and off behind him.

"Sef," I asked, "are you going to die before me?"

"Nope." He grinned. "I'm not gonna die."

I believed him.

The sky was slowly turning gray-blue now. Van slid out of bed. She padded down the hallway to the bathroom. I scooped up the stone that Sef had given me and squeezed it hard. In the dark it was a mud gray color. No blue, just the bottom of the ocean color. I lay there until Van came back with a towel wrapped around her head like a turban. "What are you waiting for," she asked me, "Christmas?"

"Maybe."

When I got downstairs, Van was pouring glasses of orange juice. Jack came in with his Spider-Man backpack hanging off the shoulders of his camouflage outfit. "You can't wear that again," Van told him.

"I'm going to wear it every day. Like Sef. I'm the one." Jack marched around the kitchen.

"You've been wearing it for, like, three days." She pointed to the stains on the front of his shirt.

"Every day. I'm the next guy in line."

"It's kind of disgusting."

He paraded to the refrigerator, swinging his arms.

"Come on, let me help you find something new."

"No." Jack bit into a cold hot dog. "No way. It's mine. It's my job."

We could hear Dad's footsteps. We could tell what kind of mood he was in by what he whistling. Today he wasn't whistling.

"Jack should change, Dad. He's been wearing that outfit for three days straight," Van said. "It stinks. Look at it."

Dad walked up to Jack and sniffed the air around him. "Smells okay to me."

Jack smiled. Bits of hot dog were stuck in his teeth.

"How about one last day, buddy, and then we'll peel it off you and throw it in the wash, and you can wear it again tomorrow. Deal?"

Jack nodded.

Dad shrugged at Van, then opened Mr. Coffee and took out the filter soggy with yesterday's coffee grounds.

Mom appeared out of nowhere, her voice high and cracking. "I know you don't believe me, but it's true."

"You've been wrong before," Dad said.

"And I've been right before. Don't tell me I haven't." Her face was pale, and her eyes were red and watery. "Remember Princess Di? Just a few days before it happened—it was like that."

"Don't, Grace. Not now. The kids have to go to school." He turned to us. "Your mother had one of her premonitions."

"Don't patronize me, Joe. I saw it just like it was on TV. Don't pretend I didn't." She flipped her long auburn hair over her shoulders and stared hard at us. "He blew up into tiny pieces, and the troops had to pick them up and put them in a bag—"

"Stop, Grace. Just shut up!" Dad yelled.

She left the room without another word.

"Sef's going to be fine," Dad said to us. "Don't listen to your mother."

This time it wasn't someone famous we'd heard about on TV. It was Sef. Jack started whimpering. The rest of his hot dog fell to the floor.

"Sef's fine," Van told him. "Don't cry."

"Tiny pieces," he said. "Peazes—"

Dad held yesterday's coffee grinds over the sink full of grimy plates and glasses piled up. Then he just dropped the filter in and mumbled something about being late. Dad worked for a construction company that was turning a furniture factory into condos outside of Boston, a three-hour commute each day.

He looked lost when he turned toward the door. "Be good, kids," he said, and disappeared.

We missed the bus. Van said we could have a ride in Finn's Rabbit. "Just today," she told us.

"It's not a rabbit," Jack said as we slid into the back. He rested his head on the window and made long moaning sounds that made his whole upper body shake.

"What's the matter with him now?" Finn asked Van. "He's not going to hit me over the head or anything, is he?"

Jack shook his head and moved closer to me. My legs were shaking, too.

"He misses Sef," Van said.

"Tiny peazes," Jack said softly.

Van turned in her seat and said to Jack, "Don't listen to Mom."

"Peaze train!" Jack shouted.

"He's not going to do anything crazy, is he? I mean, should I pull over?"

"No, he'll be fine."

I leaned toward the front seat. "Our mother told us she saw Sef blow up into pieces. One of her premonitions. She predicted Princess Di's car crash like two days before it happened. And JFK Junior too."

"For real?" He started laughing.

Van glared at me. That was too much information.

Finn had to pull over to the side of the road, he was laughing so much.

"What's so funny?" I asked.

"You know, you guys totally bummed me out the other day when I was over there. But *you're* crazy. Not me."

"Who's crazy?" Van looked like she didn't know whether to laugh or cry.

"Forget it." Finn wiped his eyes and laughed a little more before he stepped on the gas and pulled back on the road.

At least Jack had stopped groaning.

Mom shouldn't have said that in front of Jack. And she was wrong. I knew she was. Sef had always been lucky. It wasn't like his good luck could suddenly run out.

The day Sef turned twelve, Dad took him to the Hillview Gun Club. Dad said Sef had a really good shot. He hit everything. Some of the men there called him the Kid. Mom wasn't happy, but she didn't stop them. She did say no guns in the house, though.

One Sunday Sef came back with red eyes and went straight to his room. He didn't tell me until weeks later what had happened. A stray dog showed up at the club, a mutt. It bit one of the men when they tried to run it off. The man almost shot it, but the others told him to let the Kid do it.

"I had to," Sef told me. "They were all cheering me on."

"Why'd you have to?"

"I wanted to go back there, Cass. I love shooting with Dad."

"What'd Dad say?"

"Nothing. He didn't say anything. Didn't tell me what to do either way. Better not tell Mom or Van either."

"You really did that?"

"Yeah." He was quiet, then his eyes got wet again. "The stupid dog had three legs, Cass. And the worst part was he looked at me right before I did it. I think it's gonna be bad luck."

"Maybe," I said. "What'd they do with it?"

"The dog?" He backed away from me then, and I thought, *I don't know this Sef.*

Sef was going to come back home. He had to. He couldn't die. But then it struck me that I'd only been thinking all this time about if Sef was killed. What if he killed someone else? He might have to. I knew then that when Sef came back, he wouldn't be the same person.

WHAT A WASTE

JACK WAS QUIET the rest of the way to school. Finn dropped us off at the elementary school entrance, and he and Van kept going down the road to the high school. The middle grades had their own wing on the other side of the school from the kindergarten to fifth-graders. I took Jack to his special-needs class, then ran to the main office for a late slip.

On the first day of school, the sewer had seeped into the hallway, leaving a stink in the entire middle school hallway. It still seemed to be there. I stared at the fluorescent panels of light along the ceiling of the hallway all the way to social studies. On the door there was a poster of different-colored ice cream cones. It said SUCCESS COMES IN MANY FLAVORS. HAVE A SCOOP. I was already late, and for a minute, I thought about not going into class at all. No one would have said anything. I got all A's.

Mr. Barkan was writing on the chalkboard. He had on his usual too-short brown polyester pants, white socks, and clunky brown shoes. I dropped the pink slip on his desk. Sonia glanced at me as I passed her. She had on lots of makeup and a new tight black T-shirt that said SWEET. I couldn't remember if I'd brushed my hair this morning. My best friend seemed like a stranger. Or maybe I was. But somehow I felt like nothing more could hurt me.

As I took my seat, Kimberly Love turned to me and whispered, "Did Sef leave?"

Everyone called her Big Mouth Kim. She was half Japanese and had a long dark braid and glasses. Her brother Don was a friend of Sef's. A senior this year, he was about the best basketball player Hillview ever had.

"Yesterday morning."

"I'm sorry."

"Thanks." I looked down.

"Don would have gone to the party, but he wasn't here—"

"Girls, do you have something you want to tell all of us?" Mr. Barkan was chewing on the end of his glasses.

Kim and I looked at each other.

"Is it more important than the War of 1812?" he asked.

That only happened about a million years ago. "Yeah, it is," I said, surprising myself.

Laughter rocked the classroom back and forth.

"That so?" Mr. Barkan said. "Well, Cassie, you can tell me all about it after class. All right, everyone, eyes up here. Washington's advice to the country was that we should steer clear of permanent alliances with the foreign world—"

Sonia was smiling to herself. I remembered her saying, "Everything's always about Sef." I closed my eyes, and the world became white noise.

I stayed after class. Mr. Barkan said, "You were disrespectful.

You're setting the wrong example. Okay?" He crossed his hands over his chest. "Do you have anything to say?"

Tiny specks of spit were coming out of the corners of his mouth. I suddenly felt sorry for him.

"Well, can we talk about something more recent? I mean, what about the Iraq War?"

He nodded. "Okay. We can do something like that. Is your brother there?"

"He left yesterday," I said.

"Okay, okay. We'll figure something out. Go ahead to your next class."

"Thanks."

"Hello, earth to Cassie. Did you do your paragraph on *The Giver*?" It was Big Mouth Kim, waiting in line for school lunch.

"No, I forgot."

She leaned against the wall, her fingers tapping the Girl Power Got Milk? poster. "9 Essential Nutrients to Help You Perform Your Best." She pointed to the poster. "That's why I'm getting chocolate milk. Where have you been going to, anyway?"

"The library." Last week I started taking my lunch there instead of sitting at Sonia's table.

"Oh, that's cool. Do you want to sit with me today?"

She wore Converse sneakers, one red and one black, jeans, and a sweatshirt with the sleeves cut off. She'd always dressed a little weird. But I liked her style—better than what Sonia and all the other girls were wearing. I shrugged and carried my tray to the far seat by the window. "Sure."

She followed me. "What's up with you and Sonia?"

The last person I was planning to tell anything to was Big Mouth Kim. "Nothing." I sat down. "Just a stupid fight."

She nodded and opened her Hello Kitty lunch box.

"What is that?" I asked.

"Cabbage and carrot and radish on fried noodles with egg." She held up the plastic container. "Want to try some?"

"No, thanks."

Sonia's new best friend, Michaela, stopped at our table. For years, Sonia had made fun of her for being such a princess, but not anymore. Michaela straightened her hair every week at a salon and wore a diamond ring because her father owned a jewelry store. She looked from Kim to me and back. "What business are you doing for math?" she asked Kim.

We were all in the same English class, but only I was in advanced math. I used to help do Michaela's homework for her during lunch.

"What's the assignment?" I asked.

"You have to plan and budget a new business," Kim said. She turned to Michaela. "Mine's organic farming."

"For real?" Michaela said.

"Yeah."

"You think you can actually make money selling carrots and peas and stuff?" Michaela lifted her eyebrows.

"What's yours?" Kim asked.

"I have my own line of clothing."

"Like JLo?"

"I'm totally not doing perfumes." Michaela smiled. "Mine is more like Gisele's."

"Right." Kim ate a forkful of vegetables and noodles.

I ate the blob of whipped cream off my green square of Jell-O. It melted in my mouth. Then I bit into my sloppy joe oozing with tomato.

"Are you going to eat that? Do you, like, even know where that meat came from?" Michaela asked.

"China?" I asked. "Doesn't everything come from China?" Kim laughed.

"Very funny," Michaela said. "When you start rolling around the ground dying, don't say I didn't warn you."

"No one else has died, so I guess I'll risk it."

"Whatever," Michaela said, and walked away.

"Whatever," Kim mimicked. "Maybe she should go to Iraq. Did you know I have a cousin there? In Iraq."

"You do? Is he okay?"

"Yeah, he's okay."

"Thanks," I said.

"For what?"

"Just thanks."

I was the first one in English class. In black jeans and T-shirt, Mr. Giraldi looked up at me and smiled. Before he came to the middle school, he taught at the high school. Sef was in his class. Everyone liked Mr. G. He was young and pretty cool, and there was the cute factor. Some of the girls had crushes on him.

"I don't have my paragraph," I told Mr. G. "I couldn't really do anything. Sef left yesterday."

"All right, no problem. Don't worry, okay? Sounds like you have a lot going on right now." Then he sighed and muttered, "What a waste."

"What's a waste?"

His eyes blinked shut, then opened. "Listen, Sef's a good kid. I hope to God he's safe. Try to do your work tonight."

I nodded. *What a waste.* Sef?

I sat down, watching everyone like they were on a screen in front of me. I was far, far away.

"All right, everyone, eyes and ears please. Let's review *The Giver* before we talk about your paragraph on memory. In Jonas's utopia, there are no choices, no pain or fear. There is no access to memory. What would we be without our memories, without our past?"

"Zombies?" Brandon said.

A few kids laughed.

"That'd be so cool," Sonia said. "I mean, like, no pain? Ever?"

"Aren't utopias perfect? They probably didn't have homework there either," Kim said.

"Okay, you have a lot of ideas. Let's get on track. I want to do a little brainstorming. Remember back to your first day of school in September, a whole two months ago, and write your thoughts. Fears, joys, expectations, whatever comes to mind—"

"The only thing I was afraid of was how much homework they said you'd give us," Kim said.

"Kim, you're talking while I'm talking. Write it down. Whatever you experienced, good or bad."

I stared at my sheet of paper.

"Five minutes, just write."

Through the window I could see the field hockey field. The sun was bright, and the sky was blue. I wrote on the top of my paper "My First Day of Seventh Grade, September 6, 2006: The

Day the Sewer Overflowed in the Hallway." It seemed like so long ago. Sef was at boot camp.

Early that morning, Dad had knocked on our door. "Who's ready to roll?"

"Not Van," I said. I was sitting on my bed in jeans and a T-shirt watching Van try on outfits.

"I can't decide what to wear," she moaned.

"What's wrong with what you have on?"

"It looks stupid."

"No it doesn't," Dad said.

"Yes it does."

"She thinks the skirt makes her look fat," I said.

"Oh, Van. You're not fat." He put his hand on his belly. "If you just wore the same thing every day like me and Cass, you wouldn't have this problem."

"Thanks. That's helpful."

Dad shrugged and looked at me, and I shrugged back.

"Cass," he said, pointing to my window, "what happened to your flag?"

After 9/11, Dad got us each little flags on stands for our rooms. "It fell down," I said, which was pretty much true. It fell down because I knocked it down the day Sef left for training.

I said, "Dad, I don't want Sef to go."

"You sound like your mother."

Van laughed.

I turned to her. "What? You want him to go?"

She stopped brushing her hair. "No."

"Then why don't you ever say anything?"

"Listen," Dad said, "it's his decision, and he's protecting our country. We have to honor the fact that he's going."

"Well, I don't," I said.

Downstairs, Mom called, "Breakfast!"

"Do you know what Sonia's dad told Mom?" I asked.

"What?"

"That he was for the war, but he'd never send his own kid."

"That figures." Dad took a sharp breath, straightening his shoulders and puffing out his chest. "He told Mom that? He should have told me."

"I bet you could still talk Sef out of it."

"It's not exactly up for discussion, Cass. He's going to defend his country."

"From what?"

"From terrorists."

"In Iraq? I thought bin Laden was in a cave in Afghanistan or Pakistan or somewhere."

"Terrorists are everywhere. Listen"—he pointed at me— "you better hurry up and get downstairs before your mother turns into a terrorist. And your flag's going back up."

When I left that morning, I saw it standing in my window— the little flag that didn't wave or flap or make a sound.

"All right, who wants to share their fears, hopes, and expectations of their first day of seventh grade? What memories have you come up with?" Mr. Giraldi asked.

Hands went up. Whoever Mr. G threw his orange ball to had the floor. He wasn't going to throw it to me. I drifted out. But when everyone started laughing at Brandon, I laughed too.

He threw the orange ball to Michaela. Under her sweater, her T-shirt said I'M NOT SHORT. I'M FUN SIZE. "Whoa, Michaela's got the floor. Go."

"I was so nervous on my first day. I mean it was, like, seventh grade. I did the most embarrassing thing, I can't even say it." She giggled.

"Did you make the septic overflow?" someone asked.

"No way!" Michaela turned red. "But who wants to have bad memories? That's crazy."

"Okay, how do others feel? Is having no memories better than having bad memories? In a way, they're like our history. How do memories make us who we are?" The orange ball flew across the room.

What if Sef went away and I had no memory of him? Would that be better? What if I couldn't see his face anymore or remember him running beside me or even miss him? What if he just disappeared?

Next thing I knew, Mr. G was throwing the orange ball up and catching it as he told us our homework for tomorrow. "I'll take your memories before you go."

Everyone started streaming out. Brandon tripped and fell in the doorway.

"Brandon, if you pulled your pants up, you might have an easier time walking."

They laughed as they turned in their memories. I folded up my nearly blank page and put it in my pocket.

CHAPTER 8

THE DEAL

WHEN JACK AND I got home, Mom was on the couch watching soap operas with the phone in her hand. Jack dropped his backpack on the floor, turned around, and went back outside.

"Why are you home?" I asked Mom.

Mondays, Wednesdays, and Fridays, she worked as a receptionist at a dentist's office in town. Dr. Hoffman was always chewing gum and telling bad jokes. Once he cleaned only half my teeth. Since we got our teeth done at a discount, we never said anything.

She didn't answer me. The breakfast dishes were piled up in the sink, and the counter was covered in coffee cups, eggs, and bread. Old photo albums were stacked on the kitchen table. I put the food away and put the dishes in the dishwasher and wiped down the counter. Through the door, I saw Jack sitting under the chestnut tree in the backyard looking up into the leaves.

"Do you still want me to watch Jack?" I asked Mom.

"If you want to."

"You can since you're home," I said, and went upstairs and lay on my bed, using my backpack of books as a pillow. So much homework had piled up from last week. I had to study for math and science tests, read *The Giver*, and write my paragraph. Osmosis, I thought. My brain would absorb it all as I slept.

When I woke, it was dark out. I saw the outline of Van's body bent over the computer. She never took naps, ever. She turned to me.

"I take it Sef didn't call," she said.

"I guess not." The words stuck in my throat. "But he's not dead as far as we know."

Her eyes widened. "Don't even say it. What's Mom doing, anyway, lying on the couch all day? I mean, why isn't she getting supper or anything? If she even brings up that stupid premonition again—and you don't have to tell people either, like you did this morning. Everyone will think she's totally crazy."

"She is crazy."

"He's only been gone for a day, and it's like a morgue in here. I mean I miss him, too, but we still have to do everything. We have to eat." She slid her chair back. "I'm going to get something for supper."

By the time I made my way down, Van was making her way back up with a salad. I could hear Jack down in the kitchen singing, *"E-I-E-I-O."*

I started making a deal then. If Mom's premonition was wrong and Sef was fine, then I'd be good. I really would. It wasn't like I was bad, but I would have to stop being so mad at Mom, for one.

I didn't know exactly whom I was making a deal with as I looked up at the sky and said it. *Swore* it.

On the table next to Mom was a bottle of wine. The weather lady was talking about a cold front coming down from Canada.

"Do you want something to eat, Mom?" I asked.

"Moo moo here, and moo moo there—" Jack sang.

"Can we make pancakes?" I asked.

Still she didn't answer. In the kitchen, Jack was holding the refrigerator door open, staring in at the white light. "Moo moo and moo moo—"

"Go ask her if we can make pancakes," I told him. "She'll say yes to you."

In a minute, Jack came back smiling.

I already had the Bisquick in a bowl. "Get the chocolate chips," I told him. We added the whole bag and started eating spoonfuls of the batter while the frying pan heated up.

The phone rang once. I ran to the living room just in time to see Mom drop the receiver and then pick it up. It was Dad calling to say not to wait for him.

When we were done eating, Jack and I went up to Sef's room. Jack lay on top of Sef's bed, his face and hands sticky with maple syrup, his clothes grass-stained and caked with dirt. Bits of leaves were stuck in his hair.

"White Kitty," he said.

I brought his kitty, and he closed his eyes.

On the back of Sef's door was a dartboard of Osama bin Laden's face. You got one hundred points if you hit him between the eyebrows, fifty for his face, and twenty-five for his beard. We had laughed at bin Laden before, but now when I looked into his black eyes, I was afraid.

I pressed Play on Sef's CD box. The song started in a soft guitar. A deep bass sounded next and then something ominous. A thumping, like out of a scary movie. Then the voice came in: *Did did did did you see the frightened ones*— I hit Stop and went over to Jack with his mouth open, snoring, and White Kitty tucked under his chin.

I spread Sef's blue comforter on Jack, rolled him over, and lay down beside him. Just below the headboard, the wallpaper was peeling off. The silver airplanes were curling up as if they were driving into each other. I tried to stick the paper back to the wall, but it was old and dry and kept coiling off. Jack's stomach rose and fell. Outside the world was black.

I pressed Play again. *Did did did did you hear the falling bombs?* Behind the music I could hear planes whooshing by and bombs exploding. *Did you ever wonder why we had to run for shelter*— I'd heard Sef playing this all summer and never really listened. *Good-bye, blue sky, good-bye*—

THE COMMUNITY

I RAN IN to homeroom the next day just as everyone was standing for the Pledge. I stood and automatically put my hand on my chest, and started to say the words. Kim was next to me, and I heard her say "and to the Republic for Richard Stands: one Nation under blah blah with discrimination and war for all." She smiled at me, and I smiled back. Had she been saying this all this time, and I never heard it until now?

She leaned toward me. "What happened to your sister?"

"Nothing. Why?"

"I saw her crying after school yesterday."

"Van? You did?"

"Yes." Kim's dark eyes stared into mine, waiting.

"Where was she?" Van seemed the same as always last night.

"At the basketball court at Dana Park, watching Finn and some other guys shooting hoops. I was looking for my brother. I saw a bunch of them get in a car, a blue wagon, I've seen down there before. Van was in there for a couple minutes. Then she jumped out and ran up the hill, and she was crying."

Sef and I played at Dana court. Van never went there. "You sure?" I asked.

The first bell rang.

"I'm sure. I can try to find out something, but no one tells me anything. They think I have a big—" She pointed into her open, smiling mouth.

Mr. Barkan's glasses hung from the corner of his mouth as he paced in between the aisles. "It's been brought to my attention that we don't do much with current news in our class."

As he walked by me, I stared at my desk. *LEAH 2002* had been scratched into the top with pen.

"So, in addition to what we're studying, I want each of you to find a blog written by someone you're interested in learning more about. It should be about someone from another country, and it might be fun if it's someone your age. Read about them, find articles on their country in the paper."

Dave Swanson, the math genius of seventh grade, asked, "Is this a mandatory assignment?" He was tall and skinny with a crew cut and freckles. He hadn't spoken to me since last year when I said I couldn't go to the Spring Dance with him. Of course, I hadn't given him much chance to talk to me either.

"Yes. See how they live their lives. Take notes on their culture and traditions. Email them. Print pictures. We'll present reports based on your correspondences and research. You have a week to find a site.

"Now, back to where we left off yesterday. The War of 1812." Mr. Barkan pulled down one of the maps rolled like a window shade over the chalkboard. It snapped back up into his face before it coiled tight again. A few people in the back laughed. He smiled and shook his head.

In the cafeteria, I passed Sonia's table. She was wearing skintight jeans and a white shirt that said HOT in red letters under a gray hoodie. I knew she saw me. Her high-tops went *tap tap tap*, and her lips curved up. Once Sonia told me that she liked me because I wasn't like everyone else. I hadn't changed. She was the one who'd changed. She was just like everyone else now. She didn't look up as I walked by with my tray. I felt a little ache in my stomach. I missed her—the old Sonia.

Kim was reading *The Giver* at her table. She was almost finished. I sat down, said hi, and opened my book. She leaned across the table and whispered, "I had a dream about Mr. G last night."

"No way."

She nodded and cupped her hands on either side of her mouth. "Yes."

"Details, please."

"I don't think so."

I laughed. "I would never tell my dreams like Jonas does. Not in a million years." In *The Giver*, Jonas told his family his dreams and his strongest feelings. They were analyzed and compartmentalized, put away or taken care of with a pill.

"Me neither. My mom would probably schedule an appointment with a shrink or something."

The bell rang. We shut our books and walked to English class.

Mr. Giraldi walked in and out of the desks, holding *The Giver* behind his back. "All right, so let's talk about Stirrings today."

A few giggled. Someone groaned.

"What do you think? When Jonas feels his first Stirrings in his dream about Fiona, do you think they should be controlled by a pill?"

"Rob wants to talk about his Stirrings," Jesse said.

Rob smacked Jesse on the back. They had been best friends since the day Rob moved to Hillview a year ago. Both were tall and lanky and good-looking. While Jesse had blue eyes and light skin, Rob had dark eyes, and his skin was the color of Mom's coffee after she poured in half-and-half. It was hard not to notice them as they moved down the hallway, joking and laughing, tossing a ball back and forth.

When he came into our social studies class the first time, Rob had on his usual flannel shirt and black jeans. He looked around the class at everyone, and I swear his eyes stopped on me. It seemed like he actually *saw* me. I liked him, but so did all the other girls in our grade, so I didn't think about it much. A few of them had asked him to go to the Spring Dance, but he said no. Last summer they had come to the Dana Park basketball court where Sef and I were shooting. We played HORSE. It was easy to be with them when Sef was there.

"All right, take it easy, boys," Mr. G said. "Let's stick to the book."

Kim raised her hand, and Mr. Giraldi threw her the orange ball. "I think it's creepy. I mean he has a dream about a girl, and he has to take a pill? They control everything. And only

Birthmothers have babies and then they have to be Laborers for the rest of their lives? What's that say about mothers?"

"All right, good point, Kim. What do others think?"

"Can I say one more thing?" Kim asked.

"Go for it."

"It's weird that everyone is the same. They do everything the same every year. I mean, no one is different."

"You wouldn't be there," Brandon called out.

"All right, Brandon, so tell us what kind of society this is," Mr. Giraldi said. Kim threw him the ball hard.

"It's like this perfect place. But you don't even pick what job you want to do."

"But it's safe," I interrupted, without raising my hand. "There's no war. No confusion. Things are easy. Everyone's normal and healthy."

Brandon held the ball up in his fist. "No freedom either!"

"All right, there are a lot of good points here. Who's making all the decisions in the community?"

"The Committee of Elders," I said.

"Ball," Mr. Giraldi said, pointing to me.

Brandon threw it to me sidearm.

"Cassie?"

"At least in their community there aren't people blown up and walking around without arms and legs or whatever. There isn't even a reason to go to war there." My voice was getting louder. I couldn't stop it. "They probably don't even have a word for war."

Everyone looked at me.

"All right, everyone is normal and safe. What's most important? Safety and sameness or freedom and individuality?"

"Where do all the old people go when they're released?" Sonia blurted out. "I mean, do they just, like, go away all of a sudden?"

"It's just a nice word for time to die," Kim said. "As in execution."

"Disgusting," Lisa said.

My insides went cold. Of course that's what it meant. When I read it the first time, it sounded so nice and easy—*released*. I found the stone inside my pocket. Usually I left it under my pillow. I held it in my fist. A folded-up piece of paper landed on my desk. In neat small letters, it said, *What is your email? Kim.*

"All right, let's make a list of pros and cons of the community. And then we'll talk about being released." Mr. Giraldi turned to the blackboard.

I wrote my email on a tiny square of paper, folded it in half twice, and tossed it to Kim. It landed on her lap. Then I made my own list. Pros: No war, no pain, no confusion. Sef stays. Cons: Everyone is normal, or they are released. I realized then that there would be no Jack. He was special. He was slow. He'd be released.

CHAPTER 10

RETARD

"SEF CALLED!" Mom sang out when I walked in the door. "He was in Kuwait, going to Iraq tomorrow. He's fine—he sounded just like he always does!"

"Guess he's not dead." I smiled.

"He just got there." She stirred a wooden spoon in a pot on the stove that smelled of basil, garlic, and tomato. "He said he'd be home before we knew it and wished I could send him some meatballs." She laughed and wiped her eyes with the edge of her apron. "Let's put together a care package tonight. Energy bars and chocolate should be fine. Cookies might make it."

"What else did he say?"

"He asked if you went running."

"He did? What'd you say?"

"I said yes." She looked up at me. "Did you? You know I don't want him to worry about us. He has enough to worry about over there."

"I didn't go running. But I will. I'm going to do everything I can so Sef doesn't have to worry about me over there. You should too, Mom." I looked at her hard. "So he doesn't worry about you."

The steam from the sauce rose up around her face. She stirred, tasting the sauce, not looking at me.

"Where's Jack?" she asked.

"I don't know."

Mom set down her wooden spoon. She pushed her lips into a smile. "Can you find him for me? I want to tell him about Sef. That he's okay."

The air was cold, and Jack wasn't anywhere. I walked around the chestnut tree in the back and then checked the garage. He sometimes liked to rock in his old car seat. I listened for his singing, but all I heard was the gentle *flap slap flap* of the giant flag at the end of the road. I decided to try the Adamses' yard.

Jack was sitting on the grass at the edge of the woods with their cat, Tigger, on his lap. Tigger looked too terrified to do anything. As quietly as I could, I walked up behind Jack. I would hold his hands and arms, pry them slowly away from Tigger, and then lift Jack up in a bear hug, with my chest pressed close to his back, and move him toward our yard. I knew that someday he'd be stronger than I was and I wouldn't be able to do this, but I could do it now.

I was almost behind Jack when Ben Adams ran around the side of their house yelling, "Hey, what do you think you're doing to my cat, retard?"

Jack didn't move.

"I said let her go, retard!"

Jack stared back at him.

I'd seen Ben tie sneakers to Tigger's tail when his friends were over and stick peanut butter in her mouth.

"Nice outfit. Are you in the army too?" Ben laughed.

"Marines," Jack said.

"Don't laugh at him and don't call him retard, or I'll kill you," I said, stepping in front of Jack.

"Oh, I'm scared." He was two years younger than I was, but he was big for his age.

"Let go of the stupid cat, Jack," I said.

"No, and she's not stupid."

"Let her go."

"No."

"I'll get you White Kitty," I whispered in his ear. I knelt down and put my hands on his, but he only pressed harder into Tigger. The fur rose on her back.

"I'm watching out for her," Jack said.

"What, you're the big cat protector?" Ben laughed.

"I'm the one."

Ben suddenly pushed Jack in the chest with his open palms, sending Jack back into me so both of us went sprawling onto the grass. Tigger rocketed into the woods.

"Listen, don't go touching my cat again," Ben said.

Jack jumped up and shouted, "Wait until Sef gets back. He's going to blow you away. He has guns and bombs and everything. And I'm in charge while he's gone."

"Okay, whatever you say. And don't you mean *if* he comes back?" He laughed harder.

I sprang up and jumped on him. My arms went around him in a second, knocking him off balance. I rolled him over onto his belly, pinning his arms behind his back. I had lots of practice holding Jack when he lost control, and I was stronger than I looked.

"Just shut up, okay, do you hear me? Shut up," I said.

He nodded just a little.

"Yes or no?"

"Yes," he whined.

"And don't call Jack a retard again either." I pushed Ben once and then let him go. I turned to Jack. "Let's go. Mom has something to tell you."

"I was doing my job," he said as we started back. "Tigger likes me. Am I going to get in trouble?"

"No. I probably will." Goose bumps suddenly blossomed on my arms and legs. Someone was watching me. I turned back to their house and saw Kristen Adams smirking at us from the upstairs window. I waved at her—a dismissive wave, as if I didn't care that she'd seen us. But my head became instantly heavy thinking about what she was going to say about us in school tomorrow.

"Why'd he call me retard?" Jack asked.

"Because he's an idiot. He doesn't know anything about anything." As we walked into our yard, a blue space opened like a hole in the clouds, and the sun shone on us.

"He doesn't know anything about anything," Jack repeated.

"That's right. Now let's go see Mom."

I knew one thing. I wouldn't have done what I did if Sef were home. I would have let him take care of it. That's what I used to do. Like the time we were at Swallow River and some boys we didn't know were swimming.

Sonia, Jack, Sef, and I were there that day. It was late afternoon, and the air was hot and heavy. Sef was with his friends on the other side of the river. I heard some boys laughing and turned to see Jack with his bathing suit pulled down around his ankles. There were four of them egging him on. They looked about fifteen. Jack smiled at them, like he got the joke, too.

"Jack," I yelled, "pull up your shorts!"

By this time, Sef was charging across the water. He jumped on the boy closest to Jack and started pounding him.

"What the hell? He didn't do anything!" a skinny one yelled, while the other two guys took off.

Sef stopped. "I'll kill you both, I swear. Get out of here before I do."

The kid that Sef hit staggered back. "I'll call the police if you touch me again."

"Not if you're dead, you won't." Sef turned to Jack. "Pull 'em up, Jack."

"Come on, let's go," the skinny kid said to his friend.

Jack tried to pull up his bathing suit, but the wet made it stick to his legs. I wanted to turn away, but I couldn't. Jack was crying now.

Later, though, when we got home, Jack yelled to Dad how Sef almost killed a bunch of guys at the river. He laughed and said it proudly.

"Did they deserve it?" Dad asked.

"Hell, yeah," Jack said.

Now it was my turn to watch out for Jack and the rest of us.

CHAPTER 11

I CAN NOT BREATHE

WHEN JACK AND I got home, I went to check my email to see if there was anything from Sef. Van and I shared a computer, which meant if she was home, she got it first and I got it second. There was a new email from Kim, with a list of blogs for the school assignment, written by people who lived in Iraq. I didn't want to read anything right now, especially about the war. But one of the blogs she listed was called Blue Sky, just like the song I listened to on Sef's CD player.

The Blue Sky home page was deep blue with a bright yellow sun. Under the sun it said "Hope is the thing with feathers." The blog profile said she was a thirteen-year-old student living in Baghdad. Her sign was Aquarius. There was a list of all her previous entries, going back a month. I clicked on her most recent entry.

November 19, 2006

H. and I sleep in living room until the hole is fix in our room. Today I got up early and took my breakfast. I have to get to school on time for exams. I can not walk anymore. We have to go over a bridge and checkpoint it is to dangerous. A girl was kidnapped last week and there are car bombs, helicopters, guns. My parents say they will ask for my name to see Shiite or Sunni. I am both and also my family has Kurd, Turk and German. A driver take me to school. In the morning I wait for him.

I try to eat but I was nervous for my geography exam. Mama tell me to relax and I will receive high mark fine. She say I should eat if I want to study well. I try but I am shaky. Then we heard shots close by. They keep coming. I counted twelve in one minute.

I lift the curtain even though Mama say not ever to open curtains. The man is close. I see his black pant and white shirt. He is crouched behind a car in front of Abu A.'s house. The police station is one street away. Every day it is a target. Mama come and pull down the curtain. She say to move away from the glass. I tell Mama I check for my driver. The same second someone yells outside a terrible yell. Next Mama lift the curtain to look.

Abu A. is there on the sidewalk holding his leg. Rolling side to side. The gun is disappeared. Blood pours onto the sidewalk everywhere. My mouth doesn't work. I can not breathe or talk. All is black and then I see Mama running to the kitchen for cloths. Outside Abu A. holds his leg. I follow Mama like a zombie. She is a doctor. She wraps cloths around his leg tight. It is so quiet I can hear Mama breathing. There is more blood than you can believe. Blood turns the cloths red in one second. I spread the cloths over the sidewalk to cover the blood. I do not know why I do this—I do not want to see all the blood. It helps nothing. I can not be a doctor.

Abu A. falls back and I think he is dead. Mama tells me to go see if anyone is at his house. Then R. drives by and sees what happened. He take Abu A. in his car to the hospital. We do not know yet how he is and what happened. He could die from blood lossed. What if it take too long with the checkpoints or there is no room for him in the dirty hospital?

I arrive at school in time for exam but while I should be thinking on questions, I keep on seeing the blood from Abu A.'s leg.

Mom cry for Abu A. family and S. family today and not the baby in hospital. What happened to our neighborhood? Our city? Our country? Nowhere is safe. Maybe the moon. I wish the war end and soldiers go back and Iraq to be the same again. We all pray to Allah for this.

Good-bye,

Blue Sky

I scrolled down to her photos. There weren't any of Blue Sky, just some of the inside and outside of her house with a garden in the back, a hose, and a soccer ball. Inside her house reminded me of my grandmother's, with its ornate rugs, long couches around the TV, and flowery drapes that fell to the floor and shaded the room. Like me, she had a younger brother, and she shared a small bedroom with her older sister. Blue Sky's desk had a radio, boxes, candles, pictures of friends, books, flowers in a vase, nail polish, and stuffed animals. She was like Van the way she organized everything so neatly. I wondered if she was perfect and pretty with long dark hair, like Van. She was like me in that she panicked and couldn't breathe sometimes. I didn't know anyone else this happened to.

There were a bunch of pictures of the food they served on their religious holiday, Eid. Underneath the pictures were the names of the dishes: eggplant casserole, sumac salad, beef and lamb kebabs, white bean stew, rice, lentil soup, breads, date balls, cookies, and fruit nut chocolate fudge.

The newest pictures were of her house, taken after an explosion. Windows were shattered, doors had fallen off their hinges, dishes were broken on the floor, and drapes were ripped and torn. Broken toys and pieces of metal and plastic littered the yard.

I clicked on her previous blog entry.

Blue Sky's Blog

November 14, 2006

    S. and her family left for Syria and then to Germany today. Before they left one bizarre thing happen which make me think S. can not go. Mortar fell into our ceiling just before morning prayers and I woke with a big peace of stone on my bed. I yelled for Mama to hurry quick. Everyone come to see and no one can believe it. I have not a scratch. Not one thing. H. stares at me from other bed. She can not believe her eyes. What if E. sleep in my bed with me? I pray to Allah and say thank you many time.

Our city, our school, neighborhood, and house is absent of safety. We stay home all the time except for school. The only place I visit was S.'s house. Because it was close. Her family received a threat so they have to go.

I decide not to tell about the stone on my bed when they stop at our house with their driver to leave. They have enough to worry and it was hard to talk with many crying. When I see S. I did not recognize her in the hijab she was wearing. She is Christian and never wear one. Her Mama and sister also. It is better for travel.

I cried and cried and could not stop. Mama spill water on the street after they drive away for safe trip. I spill so many tears I think more than the water from Mama. S. and I spend time together since we were babies. We study and talk about life and make homemade work like macramé. Before we all begin to lose everything. All the good people leave Iraq.

Mama took me to the hairdresser later in the morning to cheer me. All they talk about is the bombs and who is killed or moving and that make me cry all over again. R. my favorite who fix Mama's hair give me a hug and a candy.

I am very sad today.

Our electricity is off much time. I hear George Bush posted notice that electricity was restored for most Iraqis! Maybe he come here and discover. Maybe he bring S. back.

I want my life back. . . . . .I want to live. . . . . Can anyone hear me?. . . . . .

. . . .
. . . .
. . . .

Blue Sky

Blue Sky's Blog

November 12, 2006

We take some days off cleaning. I am glad. I hate cleaning and dishes. Mama took a Valium and went to bed early like she do every night since horror at the hospital. I tell you. One week past she deliver a healthy baby boy. One hour after she left the room the hospital was bomb because some people angry that American soldiers hand sweet to children. In the evacuation Mama saw her mother patient was dead. What will happen to that baby she say over.

I used to have much optimism. At first we give American soldiers Dulma and other special dishes but now we ask them to leave. I thought it would be utopia after the American solders came—like amusement park or something. But it is not. We stay inside most of the time. Some nights I sleep in the living room together with my whole family because we have many windows and they shake much.

I miss old Iraq. From the window I can see the cafe. I believe in good and nothing bad happen to us. But terrorists multiply faster than good. They say what they do is for God but they are liars and they use God. This is not our religion.

I wait for the next thing.

Impossible to no anything.

H. and I watch TV until the electricity goes out. We light candles and sit in the dark for a while. We decide to play Life. Special version for us. H. say instead of getting cars and children and jobs we get bombs and tanks and home invasions. The American version, H. laugh. They liberate us from electricity, running water, schools, safety. That's life. Ce la vie. H. laugh a lot and I to. My chest hurt still because we did not laugh for a long time.

H. stop and say it is not really funny but I can not stop laughing. We went into the kitchen and eat a cake and then feel OK to go to bed.

My bed is too small but E. is asleep in there some time and I am glad. I do not want to sleep alone. E. is 2 and he start to say a few words. Always he watch with big eyes with big dark lashes. I pray for him to grow older.

I realize I like to write because I am afraid of being alone. Of this world. What if my family is killed and I am left like that new baby in Mama's hospital. I can not think like that. We pray everyday and believe God keeps us safe.

My life is a movie. The title is "Shock and Awe!" I wish to press rewind.

Blue Sky

Blue Sky's Blog

November 4, 2006

On the way to the fruit and vegetable stand down the road I think I don't know this Baghdad. The streets are littered with plastic bags, rice, eggshells, sandals, shirts, soda cans, newspapers. Wild dogs runs through the street. Buildings are black, wires hang down, glass piled in front of ruined stores. I have to remember my dream to live.

Before I want to be a pharmacist but now I want to make Baghdad what it was. Maybe I become an architect. I tell myself to live strong.

We see Mama's hairdresser there. She say the lemons are good today so Mama examine them.

Did you heard? R. say quiet to Mama. It is against the law for the tomatoes to lie next to the cucumbers.

Mama laugh then cover her mouth and looked at Abu M. sit beside his stack of newspapers. All be careful. You never know who listens. They talk about another family they know moving to Jordan.

Blue Sky

Blue Sky's Blog

November 2, 2006

My cousin M. encourage me to start blog. He do to. He say to write what happens to me every day. I am nervous to write. I want everyone to no Iraq, old beautiful Iraq before the war. Everyone live with fear from that day almost three years past. For the war to end is best. We pray for this.

I go to school and not more because it is danger for us. Bombs go off in the streets and markets. Snipers hide in neighborhoods. So many leave our country. Professors and doctors.

You can view my profile. I like many kinds music and reading and swimming (no more swimming now). I hopes you like my blog and email me.

Regards,

Blue Sky

Sef wasn't in charge of the bombs, tanks, and home invasions. He was helping. Fixing things. That's what he did, I told myself.

I looked up *hijab*. It was a headscarf. This was how Blue Sky lived. She was only a year older than I was. I thought of what Mr. G said: *What a waste.* This war was a waste, that's what he was talking about. Most kids in my school didn't even care that there was a war. The truth was that I didn't either until Sef went there. Reading Blue Sky's blogs made me more confused. *I didn't know anything about anything.*

CHAPTER 12

RECEIVER OF MEMORIES

THE FLAG IN Van's window fluttered as she walked by. She was standing behind me. "What're you doing?"

"You're home already?" I looked up. "I'm reading a blog by a girl from Iraq."

Van dropped her backpack to the floor and fell back on her bed. "Why?" she asked.

"Why what?"

"Why are you reading her blog?"

"I feel like it," I said.

"Well, hurry up." She rolled over on her bed. "I need the computer."

"I just have to send a quick email."

She opened her French book and rested her head on it like a pillow. I could feel her eyes on me now. "Is it because you miss Sef?" she asked.

"What?"

"That you're reading that blog."

"I guess so," I said. "Don't you miss him?"

"Of course I miss him. Just because I don't say anything doesn't mean I don't miss him. I think about him all the time."

"He called today."

"I know. Mrs. Adams called, too. What'd you do to Ben?"

I shrugged. "I didn't hurt him. I put him in a Jack. What'd Mom say?"

"She said she hoped Ben's arms felt better and that you'd be over to apologize later."

I groaned.

"You should have Jacked Kristen too," Van said.

"For the other night?"

"Yup." She laughed a little, but looked hurt. "Why do all the girls fall for the singer?"

"Supper, Cassie, supper, Cassie, supper, Van!" Jack yelled up the stairs.

We went down to the kitchen. "Where's Dad?"

"He's going to be late again. They're trying to get as much done as they can before it gets cold." Mom passed the dish of meatballs to me. "I'm going back to work tomorrow."

This meant I was back on babysitting.

"You have to go over to the Adamses' later and apologize to Ben. I'm sure he deserved whatever you did to him, but they're still our neighbors."

With his mouth full of meatball, Jack grinned and said, "She Jacked him!"

We all laughed. It felt good. It was our first supper together since Sef left, even if Dad wasn't there. For that minute, I wasn't even mad at Mom. Sef had called, and he was fine. Mom cooked dinner and was doing the best she could.

"When Sef gets back, he'll blow Ben up," Jack said.

Mom had to take a big gulp of water to keep from choking. "He can't really do that, honey," she finally said.

"What about Finn?"

"No, honey." Mom covered her mouth. "Van would be sad if he did that."

Van squinted at him.

"Let's write Sef a letter right now," I said, getting up to get some paper and a pen.

Van pushed her plate of salad and spaghetti and butter away from her.

"Aren't you going to eat anything else?" Mom asked.

"I'm not that hungry."

"Are you all right? You look a little pale."

"I feel fine." Her cell phone started ringing in the pocket of her sweater.

"This is the last time," Mom said. "Tell Finn if it happens again at supper, I'm going to take your phone for a week."

"Why doesn't she ever talk to Nora anymore?" I said. "Or Ally or anyone but Finn?"

"Peaze train," Jack said.

Van glared at us and left the room with her phone to her ear.

"Van's not going to be healthy," Jack said.

"Why not?" Mom asked.

"She didn't eat her vegetables."

"She doesn't eat anything."

"Dear Sef," I said out loud as I wrote.

Jack said, "Tell him I'm taking care of everything. And tell him about how I was taking care of Tigger and Ben came over and you Jacked him."

"Okay." I wrote slowly. "What else?"

"Tell him we're eating meatballs now," Mom said. "And that I made way too many because I forgot how many of them he always ate. And tell him we wish he was here, but we're all fine. We're all fine."

"Do you want me to write that twice?"

She laughed. "Well, no, I guess not."

After a minute I asked, "Anything else?"

"Tell him I'm never taking my uniform off, just like him."

"Well, he takes it off sometimes to wash it and take a shower." Mom frowned at Jack. "That is filthy. Tell Sef we're going to scrub Jack and his uniform pronto."

"Anyone else want to say anything?" I glanced to the living room where Van was leaning over the couch, talking. Her short skirt rode up as she shifted her weight from one leg to the other. I could see the soft curves of her thighs underneath her black tights. Her dark hair fell down her back as she rocked slightly in her tall boots.

"Van," I called, "what do you want to say to Sef?"

She snapped her cell phone shut and said, "Tell him Finn and I are getting married." She burst out laughing. "Just kidding. Tell him I miss him." She tossed her hair back and headed for the stairs.

"What's up with her?" Mom mumbled.

• • •

While Mom helped Jack in the tub, I went over to the Adamses'. They didn't ask me inside. I stood on the doorstep, and they stood under the bright hallway light, Ben between his parents.

"I'm sorry about this afternoon," I said. I was sorry, I thought, that I didn't pin him down harder.

"Ben said Jack was strangling Tigger and when he came over to save Tigger, you jumped on him," his mother said, squeezing Ben's shoulder. Kristen was standing at the top of the stairs. Her T-shirt was twisted into a knot, showing her belly.

Mr. Adams shook his head and loosened his tie. His fists opened and closed. He always seemed like he was about to explode—when he was around, anyway. Most of the time he was away on business.

"He pushed Jack first and knocked him over, and Jack wasn't strangling Tigger," I said.

Suddenly I could feel Sef nearby, smiling at me. "And Ben called Jack a retard. But I was the oldest one there, so I should have taken responsibility. So I'm sorry."

Mrs. Adams nodded and seemed satisfied with this. "All right, sweetie?" she asked Ben.

He glared at me without saying anything.

I smiled. "Better go do my homework. Good night, Mr. and Mrs. Adams, good night, Ben. Bye, Kristen."

I didn't wait for a reply. I looked up at the black sky and sprinted across their lawn. I heard Mr. Adams's voice, hard and low, "Ben, she's a girl, for crissake." I laughed and kept running fast. It was dark and the cold air smelled of smoke. I let something in my mind go and ran like I was racing Sef past the neighbors' houses, past the trees and cornfields, into the dark. Then I saw him. His head was back, his mouth was open, and he was laughing. It was like I had been given a picture of him. I held on to it.

I ran until I was just muscle and motion. My heart was beating so fast, and my legs and arms were pumping, and I went all the way to Turtle Pond. Sef was close—I could smell him, that cottony, sweaty smell. The stars blinked above, then I turned and jogged slowly back, letting my arms and legs shake out. My head felt like it had opened up and was part of the enormous sky, the same sky in Iraq—this blue-black yellow-gray sky. I thought about how I hadn't cared about anything in the past weeks. Now I did. I felt part of the world, this messed-up place without Sef. I ran faster toward home.

Finn's Rabbit was parked on the side of the road. I stopped and ducked down so they wouldn't see me. Van was inside, sitting almost in the driver's seat. Finn lifted a bottle to his mouth and drank. Then he passed the bottle to Van. She held it in front of her as if she didn't know what to do, then threw her head back and drank. When she was done, she shook her head fiercely back and forth. Her body shuddered. I couldn't see her face.

"Van," I wanted to call. "Van, what are you doing?"

When I got out of the shower, I saw Van tiptoeing back into the house. She came up the stairs and stared at me in my towel.

"I hate it here," she said. Her words hit me like stones. Then she went into our room and fell asleep on top of her bed in all her clothes and makeup.

I felt an ache inside because she seemed so far away. I unzipped her long black boots and pulled them off. I slipped them on my own feet, tucking my jeans inside like she wore them, but they looked stupid, so I took them off. I took my comforter and put it on top of Van.

I went into Sef's room. Jack was finally out of his camouflage outfit and asleep in Sef's bed with a Robert Frost book upside down on his chest. His favorite poem was "Stopping by Woods on a Snowy Evening." He couldn't read, but every night before bed he'd say the lines he'd memorized: "The woods are lovely, dark and deep, / But I have promises to keep, / And miles to go before I sleep, / And miles to go before I sleep."

I opened Sef's closet and put on the navy hoodie he used to wear all the time. I breathed it in. It still had the cottony, sweaty, spicy smell of him. Downstairs I could hear Dad talking and dishes clanging. It was almost nine, and I hadn't started my homework. I was three days behind in social studies, and we had a test coming up. Math I could do on the bus, but I had to write up a lab report for science. My heart was still racing. I picked up *The Giver* and started to read.

Jonas was going to be the Receiver of Memories. That was me, too. Pictures of Jack, Van, and Sef laughing flashed through my head. Jonas was going to know too much. Jonas had the same color eyes I had, pale blue. Something bad was going to happen to him, I knew it. He wasn't going to be a child anymore.

CHAPTER 13

WHAT HAVE YOU DONE TODAY TO WIN IRAQI HEARTS AND MINDS?

To: Blue Sky
From: Cassie
Subject: hi from USA

Dear Blue Sky,

I like your blog name. What does it mean? There's a song called "Good-bye Blue Sky." Do you know it? I read all your blogs. I'm sorry the war has made things so bad for you and your family. It's hard to imagine bombs falling and snipers shooting on the way to school. I have a brother in Iraq. You said you didn't like the American soldiers, but he is trying to make things better. He really is. I didn't want him to go, but he said he had to. He wants to make a difference.

I hope it's OK to ask you this. When your neighbor got shot, you said that you couldn't breathe or speak or do anything. This happens to me sometimes. I can't breathe, and my heart beats so fast I feel like I'm going to suffocate or drown. It's so scary. I don't know what it means, do you? (I haven't told anyone about this before!)

> I hope you write back.
>
> Cassie

To: Mom, Dad, Van, Cassie
From: Sef
Subject: I'm here!

Hi Mom, Dad, Van, Cass, and Jack,

Can't believe I'm really here. I haven't even showered yet. I heard it'll happen about once a week (yup, I'm going to stink, Mom). At least the rest of Iraq smells worse than I do. It stinks of sewage and trash and smoke, and the streets are piled with garbage.

I'm carrying about 60 lbs every day between rifles, ammo, grenades, knives, the works. Better not tell Jack about that or he'll go out and find 60 lbs of water guns to carry around. Hope you're taking care of everyone, Jack, buddy! And, Cass, are you running? Van, I hope you're doing good. I really miss you guys. I put a picture of us inside my helmet for good luck. Cass is even smiling! Remember that pic?

Not all the guys are the same as in training, but a lot of them are. Remember Hurricane, Mark, and Tim? Hurricane brought *Calvin and Hobbes* with him and a bunch of movies. He's watched *The Champ* 36 times or something. I guess he used to be a boxer. Tim has all these Metallica and AC/DC CDs that he plays all the time on his crappy little box. Mark has about a hundred bottles of hand sanitizer that his mom packed. Anyway, we're all helping each other out, watching out for each other.

There's a sign on the entrance of the compound that says, "What have you done today to win Iraqi hearts and minds?" We haven't done too much yet. Just starting to get familiar with our area of Baghdad.

My new drink of choice is Mountain Dew. We drink it all day. How's that for excitement? Better go. Hang in there. That's what we say around here. I'll write as soon as I can.

Love,

Sef

I couldn't remember which photo I was smiling in. Whichever one it was, it made me feel good that Sef had it inside his helmet for luck. I held on to my blue stone and read his email again and again.

To: Sef
From: Cassie
Subject: Re: I'm here!

Hey Sef,

Thanks for writing! Jack's definitely in a competition with you for no showers, though he may not know it. He's been wearing his camouflage every day. It's pretty gross. And just so you know, he's taken over your room. It's really weird around here without you.

Mom seems OK. Dad's been working late. Van's still going out with Finn. Surprise, surprise. He gave us a ride to school the other day. If you ask me, HE's weird. I'm good. I've been hanging out with Don Love's sister Kim. She's pretty cool.

How are you? Is your friend from boot camp there, Cali? What's it been like?

I've been listening to your Pink Floyd CD. And Kim sent me a link to a blog by this girl in Iraq, Blue Sky, so I sorta feel like I know where you are. That's all. Did you ever read *The Giver*? Write again when you can. It was great to hear from you.

Love,

Cass

SLEDDING INTO WHITE

AT LUNCH, Kristen Adams was at the next table over. She and her friends were laughing. One of them was pointing in my direction. Kim called me over. She was sitting with some eighth-graders who were studying for a test. "Want to sit down?" she asked.

"Sure," I said. "Thanks."

Kim popped a piece of fresh ginger in to her mouth. "Did you see the way Dave Swanson looked at you in social studies?"

This morning we had gone around the room telling everyone what blog we'd chosen. I said, "I chose to learn about Blue Sky, an Iraqi girl. My objective is to learn about Iraq, where my brother Sef is fighting in the war."

"I'm not sure if it was you or the war, but he was really looking at you weird. He was sort of leering," Kim said. "I mean, he almost fell off his chair."

I remembered only that my face had gone hot. "Sometimes he looks at me like that in math too. He's a little weird."

"Yeah, but he seems harmless. Maybe he wants to do math problems together."

"Can we change the subject now?" I groaned. "Thanks for sending the blogs."

"Yup. So, have you heard from Blue Sky?"

"I emailed her, but I haven't heard back."

"She probably doesn't have electricity." Kim picked up a piece of sushi with her chopsticks. "Want to try a piece?"

"I've never had it before."

She laughed. "My mom makes it all the time. Here."

"Is it, uh, raw?"

"This one's vegetable. Don't worry, it doesn't swim."

It was tangy and crispy. "It's good."

We ate for a while without saying anything. Even though Kim was big, all her gestures were slow and delicate as she ate. Her chopsticks moved like wands dancing in the air.

"I see what you mean about *The Giver* now," I said. "Imagine holding all the memories of the world? Just last week's memories were enough."

"It gets worse."

"Don't tell me."

"Have you gotten to the part where he starts receiving the memories?"

"The first ones."

"There's one about war. Just thought you'd want to know."

"Thanks for the warning."

When Kim and I got up to toss our trash, one of Kristen's friends intercepted me. "Did you really jump on Kristen Adams's little brother and almost kill their cat?"

"Not exactly."

"That's what I heard."

Kim said, "Didn't anyone ever tell you that you shouldn't believe everything you hear? It's a sign of low intelligence."

"Yeah, whatever." The girl spun around and left.

"I always think of the right thing to say when it's too late," I said. "Then I never end up saying anything."

"Well, *you're* not called Big Mouth Cass, are you?" she said. "I'll see you in English."

Michaela cornered me at my locker. Her shirt read DON'T TOUCH THE MERCHANDISE. It was such a bright neon green that my eyes blurred when I looked at it. "Why do you sit with Kim? She's so weird."

"She's not that weird. She thinks you're weird."

Michaela burst out laughing. "That's a good one. Speaking of weird, you've been really strange lately. When are you going to snap out of it?"

"Maybe tomorrow." As if I had a choice.

"Good, because I really need help with my math."

"That'll be the first thing on my list of things to do," I said.

Meg and Lisa waved to Michaela as they walked by. I glanced down the hallway. A girl's camouflage backpack caught my eye. I thought of Sef in Iraq carrying his sixty pounds of ammo, and suddenly the whole world tilted. I could see him in his uniform. I felt dizzy. My stomach rose into my chest, and I couldn't breathe right.

"I have to go," I told Michaela.

"Nice hoodie," she yelled after me. "Is it your boyfriend's?"

"Yeah, right." Sef's hoodie went all the way to my thighs.

"Maybe Dave Swanson's?" She laughed.

"Very funny, Michaela." I ran down the hallway and ducked into the entrance of the computer lab and pressed myself into the cool wall. As if I could become part of it.

I was late to English. Mr. Giraldi had written on the board, "No color, no winter, no sun, no hills, no change, everything controlled." He sat at his desk without saying anything. We sat at our desks and looked at him and each other.

"Mr. G, aren't you going to do anything?" someone asked.

Someone else whistled, which made a few others laugh.

Mr. G still didn't say anything. He rolled the orange ball across his desk.

"Mr. G, why aren't you throwing anyone the ball today?" Jesse asked.

"Yeah, this is weird," Sonia said.

"Really weird," Michaela said.

"See how used to having things a certain way we are?" Mr. G finally said as he picked up the ball. "Is it possible to forget memories? Do they ever totally leave a person as they do in Jonas's community? Let's talk."

"I have something to say," Kim said.

Mr. Giraldi threw her the orange ball.

"I wonder how much freedom we really have. I mean, I have to get up every day and go to school. I have to take certain classes and then I have to do my homework. Then get up and do the same thing the next day."

"You have a choice. You could drop out," Rob said.

"Don't think so. No one's going to drop out of my class," Mr.

Giraldi said. "How much freedom do we have? Do we all give up something for the collective good? Let's write about that tonight. One page."

There were groans across the room.

"That's what I call a collective whine," Mr. Giraldi said. He put his hand up. "Now, let's talk about the first memories Jonas receives."

The first memory Jonas received was of sledding. For the first time, he felt the cold snow on his face and the speed of the sled as he flew down the hill.

I remembered sledding with Sef when I was little. I was in the front of the toboggan, and Sef was behind me. The snow blew up in my face as we flew down the hill. The light in the sky was white behind the trees flashing by. We were sailing toward this brightness. It seemed to last forever. Either I didn't know enough to be scared then or I thought that nothing could happen to me. I wondered if that was what it was like to be Jack.

I asked Sef once what was wrong with Jack. He said, "Nothing. He's just a little slow, but he'll be able to do everything. Just you wait and see." After Jack was born, Sef was different. He used to carry Jack around in a backpack for hours every day. It was like something wasn't fair in the world and he was going to fix it. Make it better. The summer after Jack almost drowned, Sef decided he was going to teach him to swim. Every day he took him to the pond and made him paddle his legs and kick his arms. It was like he owed it to Jack. Maybe that was why Sef thought he had to go to Iraq—he felt like he owed it to someone.

While the rest of English class was talking about first memories, I opened *The Giver* and read the scene where Jonas learned about war. It was a memory of a boy soldier with matted blond hair crying out for water. He was just a boy, probably younger than Sef, and he was dying. Bleeding to death.

I stopped reading. I didn't want to know any more. When the bell rang, I sat in my chair after everyone got up and left. When Mr. Giraldi asked if anything was the matter, I said, "I can't read this book anymore. It's not fair."

"Life's not fair, is it? Just do what you can, Cassie. That's all." He put his hand on my back. Sef did that sometimes.

I ran down the hallway before I started to cry.

The next day, I told Kim that I wasn't going to finish *The Giver*.

All she said was, "Imagine having no color?"

I noticed almost everyone at Sonia's table had on some fluorescent color saying, "Look at me!" The thing about Kim was that she didn't care what I wore or if my hair and nails were done. When she took off her glasses, I thought how pretty she was. I'd never thought that before. It was strange not seeing what was right in front of me until I really looked. I told her about seeing Van and Finn.

She said, "Can you talk to her?"

"No, not really."

"Well, you can talk to me whenever you need to." She waved her chopsticks in the air. "My mom takes pills to relax. After work sometimes."

I knew I shouldn't say anything, but I did. "Mine does too. All the time since Sef left."

"I feel like I'm the adult half the time." Kim laughed. "My mother would kill me if she knew I said anything."

"Ditto. I won't say anything," I said.

"Promise?"

Big Mouth Kim was asking me not to say anything—how funny was that?

"Of course," I said.

"Well, things always get better, right?" Kim smiled.

"That's the plan." I smiled back at her. Something in my chest lifted and made me feel lighter.

CHAPTER 15

THE DEEP FREEZE

WHEN JACK AND I got home from school, Mom wasn't there. There was no message or note. I played "Good-bye Blue Sky," singing along loud. Jack sang louder, "Did did did you hear the falling bombs." I started a list of Important Things to Tell Sef because Mom said we shouldn't email him too much because he wouldn't have time to answer. I wrote:

1. I borrowed your hoodie (sorry, I'm wearing it out).
2. Do you remember sledding?
3. What are we going to do about Jack's outfit?
4. Don't bother reading *The Giver*.
5. What do you need there?

I realized right then that I could set up a donation table and send a package to Sef's team. I decided I'd ask our principal, Miss Pat, in the morning.

• • •

Mom still wasn't home at suppertime, and Jack was hungry, so I made spaghetti with butter. We were eating and watching *Tom and Jerry* when she came in. She turned off our show, put on CNN, and stood there watching in her short sweater dress and knee-high black boots, swaying side to side.

"Where were you, Mom?" I asked.

"Out with some friends." She finally turned her glassy eyes to me and Jack. "Having a good time. Is that all right with you?"

"You could have told us," I said. "We were waiting for you."

She spun around, bracing herself in the doorway, and then headed up the stairs.

"Don't you want to know if Sef called?" I yelled after her.

She stopped and turned around. "Did he?" she said, and her face went pale.

"No."

She went up to her room and didn't come back.

When Dad got home, he asked, "Where's Mom?"

"Upstairs."

"I'm starving. What'd you have for supper?" He turned on the kitchen faucet and splashed water on his face.

"Spaghetti. Want me to heat some up for you?"

"Sure. Thanks, Cass."

"With mushrooms?"

"Throw in whatever's in there."

I heated some sauce, added mushrooms, and poured it over a pile of spaghetti. I gave him a piece of baguette, and he ate and I did my homework. I liked that he didn't ask me a lot of questions that I didn't want to answer. He sopped up the last of the sauce with some bread and slumped in his chair. He glanced up at his 1994 Red Sox Championship banner and said, "Life is good, Cassie. Don't forget that."

I didn't want to tell him about Mom, but I had to. "Can I say something, Dad?"

"Shoot."

I said, "Mom's been really weird."

He leaned toward me. "Weird how?"

"We didn't even know where she was. She used to make supper every night when Sef was here. Now I don't know. It's like none of us matter or something."

Dad looked at me for a long time. Then he said, "I'm glad you told me. She's having a hard time."

"Dad," I asked, "what's the matter with her?"

"Don't worry," he said.

"I wish she'd be like she used to."

He nodded. "I know."

It wasn't fair. I pulled on my sneakers and Sef's hoodie. I needed to wash it, but it would lose the last smell of Sef if I did. I took off outside, running, gulping the cool air. I wanted to find Sef out there like I did the night I had to apologize to Ben Adams. I wanted to hear him laughing and I wanted him to fill up all that empty space inside me. But all I heard was the pounding of my own feet.

When I got back, Mom was in her bathrobe in the kitchen. Her makeup had been scrubbed off and her hair combed out. "Hi, Cassie." Her voice was cold and hard.

"Hi, Mom." I held my breath.

"Listen, I will take care of telling your father what I do. Do you understand?"

"Yes."

"Yes, what?"

"Yes, Mom."

"Good."

A Deep Freeze had begun. The next day she said good morning and then she buttoned up her lips for most of the day until she needed someone to watch Jack and then to chop some onions. Jack asked if I could take him to Dana Park. "Ask Mom," I told him. "She's not talking to me."

He frowned and marched over to Mom. "Why aren't you talking to my friend Cass?"

"Because," she said, "I'm not feeling talkative. Now go to the park."

Jack came back. "She's not feeling talkative. I think she's gonna talk to you tomorrow, Cass."

But she didn't. Not tomorrow and not the next day or the day after that.

CHAPTER 16

ONE OF
THE GOOD ONES

To: Cassie

From: Blue Sky

Subject: Re: hi from USA

Dear Cassie,

We have electricity and I write email returns. You ask me why my name and I explain. The day America started bombing Baghdad was the day the sky turned gray. The electricity go out for hours at a time and all is dark much of a day. The explosions and helicopters are more loud in the dark. When I remember old Iraq I think of light and blue sky, the color it used to be. So you understand my name now.

In my past I went to school and parties and swimming. I do nothing now and I am tired. What I want? I want to live.

I want my family to live. I try to have hope but it is difficult. I wish to have my spirit back. I wish to be a bird and fly high away. Except the sky is full with smoke and bombs.

I try to answer your questions. It is true I feel pain everyday when I hear the bombs. I feel drowning like you call. When I start to feel the panic I pray. I believe and thank Allah and live through panic. What you do?

Blue Sky

To: Blue Sky
From: Cassie
Subject: Re: Re: hi from USA

Dear Blue Sky,

Thank you for writing! I was so glad to get your email. I feel like I already know you from reading your blog. Hope you don't mind I have so many more questions for you!

I understand about your name now, but I don't understand what you are saying about the American troops. I thought we were helping. Were things better before the war? Why are we just blowing everything up?

I shouldn't say this, but I keep thinking something bad is going to happen to us. When I am panicked I try to breathe. Sometimes I have to run to breathe right again. That's what I do. I run and breathe until I am normal again.

Today we brought our grades home. My sister Van's grades went down and now she's not on the honor roll anymore. Of course my mother cried and cried about this because Van has always gotten straight A's (and Mom cries all the time about everything since Sef left). What are the girls like there? I want to know more about your life. Tell me if I write too much.

Please be safe. I wonder if there are bombs near you today. How do you sleep with the explosions?

Sef is one of the good ones. He really is. My brother Jack wishes he was a marine too. He dresses up like one every day!

> Write back, please.
> Cassie

To: Cassie
From: Blue Sky
Subject: Re: Re: Re: hi from USA

Hello Cassie,

Is your sister Van sick or hurt? In Baghdad there is no medication or therapy left for those who need it. The girls here are same. Some nice, some not nice. Now what matters most is your last name Shiite or Sunni. In past time it is not important. We live in the same neighborhood, get married, have children, all the same. No difference except how a person pray. Today they ask what is your last name and try to separate Sunnis from Shiites. Sometimes they kill the other. How do you break families apart? If true I have to kill my best friend. My uncle kill his wife. And so on. We are Iraqis—not Sunni or Shiite or Kurd or Turk or anyone.

Everything changes so much here. Before women can wear jeans and T shirt, something like that. Today clothes must cover us up. Women must wear long skirts and headscarves. Men cannot wear shorts even if they play soccer. Only pants. Before it was choice. I think the terrorist do not read the Koran. They make rules to oppress only. Where do these people come I do not no.

Before this country flow with gas. Now we line for gas. Wait 13 hours. It is crazy.

There was no Al Qaeda here before. Now terrorists are here everywhere. At beginning I talk with some soldiers. We give them water and bread. They sweat with all clothes and gear. Some give us candy back. Some talk nice. Maybe your brother Sef is one of these good ones because he is new. Three years and we are tired. We want our life. No tanks, no explosion, no guns, no raids. I try to be positive. It is stupid war. Everything blown to peaces. People lose houses, parents, children, friends.

I study now. Exams all week. Pray electricity stay so I get high marks. Pray for me this week and I pray for your family.

Blue Sky

To: Blue Sky
From: Cassie
Subject: Re: Re: Re: Re: hi from USA

Dear Blue Sky,

I read a little about the civil war there, but I don't understand it. Who started it if all the Shiites and Sunnis were living together?

I hope your exams are going well. I hope you got the

highest grades in the class. You must be busy. Do others in your class know about your blog? It's hard to believe men can't wear shorts to play soccer. What would I do? I wear jeans and T-shirts all the time.

My mother would throw a fit if she couldn't drive. But maybe she wouldn't have to worry about that because she'd never be able to wait 13 hours to get gas. Never. If she has to wait for anything for more than a few minutes, she goes crazy. It's weird, ever since Sef left, my family are like strangers. It's like I can't reach anyone. You've been through so much I know I shouldn't complain to you.

I will write again soon.

Cassie

HANG IN THERE

IN THE MORNING I went to the principal's office to ask her if we could collect things to send the troops in Iraq. She said we could start right after Thanksgiving. "We'll do whatever we can to support Sef and our troops. I'm praying for him. Every single day, I am."

"Thank you, Miss Pat," I said, and stepped back in the hallway. I wasn't going to cry, even though I felt like I'd been cut down the middle and my insides were falling out. I leaned back against the wall. I'd never be able to walk back to class.

Rob and Jesse came out of the main office. Rob put his hands up, and Jesse threw him the basketball.

"Are you busted?" Jesse asked. His Celtics shirt said PIERCE on the back.

"Not quite." I forced a smile. I was sure my eyes were glassy. Of all the times to talk to me, why was he talking to me now? "I'm going to set up a donation table in the cafeteria."

"For your brother?" Rob asked.

"Yeah." I nodded. "And the others."

"How's he doing?" Rob tossed the ball to me.

I thought about how Sef and I had beat them the time we played HORSE. I threw the ball back and started down the hall with them.

"He's all right. Says it's better than school."

They laughed. "When's he come back?"

"Not sure. It's supposed to be about a year, but they always extend the tours, I guess."

"Think he'd like a CD or something?" Rob asked.

"Yeah, I do."

"My mom would freak out if I went to Iraq," Jesse said.

"My mom *is* freaking out."

Jesse sprinted down the hall, pretending to shoot the ball.

"We have to go back to gym," Rob said. "But you should hang out at Fresh with us sometime."

Everyone had started hanging out at Fresh. They had smoothies, sandwiches, ice cream bars, and the best chocolate pie in the world.

"I'd probably have to bring my little brother Jack with me."

"That's okay. He's funny."

He knew Jack, and he still wanted us to go out with him.

"Guess I better go," Rob said. Then he stopped. "You okay?"

I nodded.

"Good," Rob said. "Hang in there."

That's what Sef said. I opened my mouth, but nothing came out. That place inside of me that was pinched and hollowed out like a cut suddenly felt smaller. My chest didn't hurt so much. It seemed to fill up with air and light. I breathed in. And out.

"Okay, see ya," I said.

After school, I was upstairs getting money to go to the corner store with Jack when the doorbell rang. The FedEx truck was parked outside. "Answer the door, Jack!" I yelled.

Downstairs was quiet.

"Jack?"

He was sitting on the couch. I asked, "Why didn't you answer the door?"

"I can't," he said softly.

"Why not?"

"Mom said I couldn't. It might be someone to tell us Sef's dead."

"She said that?"

He nodded. "She wants to answer the door."

"She really said that?"

He nodded.

"You didn't believe her, did you?"

He shook his head. "Is she crazy?"

"Come on, let's go." I grabbed his hand.

I bought a Mountain Dew at the corner store. We took swigs until it was gone. Then we tossed the bottle back and forth, laughing and running down the sidewalk. I asked Jack if he wanted to go to Fresh after school sometime. "I'll get you whatever you want. How about the chocolate pie?"

He kept looking at me. "Cass, you're like me now."

"How's that?"

"You wear the same thing every day." He pointed at Sef's sweatshirt, then looked down at his camouflage outfit.

Of course Jack would notice something that made me more like him. He once said, "You have my eyes, Cassie." I told him, "Yours are darker, Jack. See?" We stood side by side in the mirror. "No," he said. "The way they look is the same. They look far, far, far away." He said it in his high, lilting voice, and it was true.

That night as I ran I thought I heard Sef calling to me like he used to. *Cassie, Cassie.* I ran into the dark, faster and faster, trying to find him in the trees, the white of the headlights, the wind. The leaves trailed me like ghosts. If I ran fast enough, then I thought I could find him. He was out there. Was he trying to tell me something?

I was running past Sonia's when their car stopped just ahead of me. Her mother opened the window and poked her head out.

My sweatpants and sneakers were splattered with mud, and I was sweaty and gross. Susan's blond hair feathered over her shoulders, and her lips were shiny red. There was something so neat and perfect about her, like Sonia. And her father was like that too. No one would ever find any jelly or cannoli cream on the corners of his mouth or on his shirt.

"Hi, Cassie," she said. "We haven't seen you in ages. How is everyone? How's Sef?"

"Uh, he's pretty good. Says it's crazy over there, but he's doing all right," I said.

"And how's your family holding up?" Susan asked.

"We're doing all right, thanks. Hanging in there, as Sef says."

"We haven't seen you for a while." She turned to the passenger seat. I heard her say, "Sonia, aren't you going to say hi?"

Sonia half waved. She seemed so far away from me. She didn't have to imagine that someone could come to our door to tell us that Sef was dead. That was my job. She was in another world. I watched her flip her hair back and turn to the window.

"We better let you go. It's getting late. Be careful running out here in this mess." Susan smiled at me.

"I will."

I took off into the night, running like crazy, the fall air whipping on my face.

CHAPTER 18

WAR IS STUPID

ALL THANKSGIVING MORNING, Mom walked around with the phone in her hand while Dad cooked the turkey and made the mashed potatoes. Van slept all morning. I made corn muffins. There was no gravy, no stuffing, no squash with marshmallow and brown sugar. Sef was eight hours ahead of us, so by early afternoon, Mom had put the phone back in its holder. CNN blasted through the house.

When we sat down at the table, I asked, "What are we thankful for this year?"

"I'd be thankful if we could turn that damn TV off for once today. At least we could eat in some peace and quiet," Dad said.

"No," Mom said. "Please, no. It's my only connection to—"

"What about us, Mom? We're right here," Van said.

Surprised, we all turned to Van, then Mom.

Mom pointed to the TV. The CNN lady with a blond helmet of hair was saying, "One of the deadliest attacks in the entire Iraq War has killed more than one hundred and fifty people, and hundreds more are expected to be injured. A coordinated mortar and bomb attack hit a major market in Sadr City, a Shiite slum of Baghdad. Nearly one hundred fifty thousand US troops are spending Thanksgiving in Iraq far away from family—"

"I told you." Mom's face went pale. "I knew it."

"Shut the TV off, Jack," Dad said. "Don't, Grace. There are a hundred and fifty thousand troops there. He's fine."

"How do you know?"

"Believe me, I know," Dad said. "Have I ever lied to you?"

"Promise?"

"Yes. Promise."

"The war is stupid," Jack said.

Mom turned to him. Her lips pinched up. "Who said that?"

"Cassie."

"You think it's stupid too," I said to her.

"We have to respect the troops." Her voice broke. "We have to."

"Because we're blowing everything up," Jack said.

"Is that what she told you?" Mom asked.

He nodded.

"They're looking for weapons," Dad said. "They're hidden in houses, and terrorists are everywhere."

"Blue Sky says there weren't terrorists before the war," I said.

"Who's Blue Sky?" Mom tipped her wineglass to her mouth.

"A girl from Iraq who has a blog I've been reading for social studies."

"Did did did did you hear the falling bombs," Jack sang.

"Where'd you learn that?" Mom frowned.

"Sef's box."

"Well, don't sing it at the supper table, please." She turned to me. "And why do you assume everything's our fault? Why do you care about *them* so much?"

I clenched my fork. "Mom, I care about Sef more than anything in the world."

For the first time since I told Dad on her, her eyes softened when she looked at me. She was beginning to come out of the Deep Freeze. Part of me was relieved, but part of me had gotten used to the silent chill of these past weeks. It was easier not to say anything.

Dad looked like he felt sorry for me. "Sure there were terrorists. That country's always been at war, and Saddam Hussein is a mass murderer. He's wiping out the Kurds and anyone else—"

"Was," I said. "He's in jail now. Anyway, that's what Blue Sky said, and she lives there."

"Where'd she get a name like Blue Sky?" Dad asked. "And did she say anything about the plastic shredders or torturing the soccer players?"

"Joe," Mom said.

"What's a mass murderer?" Jack asked.

We all looked at him. Mom filled her wineglass.

"You don't want to know," Van said.

"Yes I do," Jack said.

"You shouldn't criticize our troops," Mom said loudly.

"She didn't say anything about the troops," Dad said. "She just doesn't have the full picture."

"I don't want to hear it. All those troops are putting their lives on the line for that country," Mom said. "Including my son."

"*Our* son. Remember? It is *our* family. I want to keep it that way." Dad turned to me. "And, Cass, as far as terrorism goes, Saddam Hussein is a terrorist. Facts are facts."

"So we should start a war in every country whose leader is a terrorist?" I was suddenly so mad about everything. I needed someone on my side. Jack didn't count. He was on everyone's side. I closed my eyes and mouth. I didn't say anything. I held on to that anger—squeezed it between my teeth. I had made a deal—I was trying to be good.

Jack ran to the TV and began to shoot with his fingers pointed like a gun. "Pow! Pow! Mom, I got the mass murderers! Sef can come home!"

"Thank you, Jack." Her eyes were watering. "I don't even know if Sef's getting something decent to eat over there."

Whatever he was having was probably better than what we were having, I thought.

"Supper, Sef, supper! Supper, Sef!" Jack called into the TV.

CHAPTER 19

NO WHERE IS SAFE

ON THANKSGIVING NIGHT I looked for an email from Sef and found a new blog from Blue Sky.

Blue Sky's Blog

November 23, 2006

A lot days past. Sorry. The electricity is very bad, on and off, most off. Two days the American soldiers broke into the shops in front of our house on the excuse to find guns. They ruined the shop where the men in our neighborhood used to sit at night to watch TV and drinking tea.

To all Americans read this: If you ever have a raid by American soldiers on your house you no nowhere is safe, not even your home. They empty drawers, turn the house upside down looking for something, put black bags on our heads. You will think again. We can do nothing. I used to feel sorry for your soldiers but not now.

Your soldiers killed my friend's brother for throwing rocks. He walked out on to the roof because it is hot. It was night and he threw rocks down so they shot him. They think he another terrorist. A nine year old terrorist! His family lose their future. I do not blame if you read this, but I tell you so you know.

I have question. Why do American think they are more than Iraqis? Our prophet Mohammed say to his soldiers not to kill any woman, child, and man, not to destroy the land. We believe this and live the way before the war.

No where is safe—not school, not street, not neighborhood, not home. Things are worse everyday. I remember how shock I was the first time I saw the majestic palm tree in our neighborhood broke in half. Three days ago I saw a dead body under that tree. It make me sick. What if I found my uncle there? I feel more sick.

I am angry, yes, and much sad this week because of my uncle. He is kidnap we think. Disappear. Taken away somewhere. No news and things become worse and worse everyday. My father is convinced he is at a torture prison. A long time to find out and not definite information or anything but we will try everything. Mom cry and cry. My little brother stares at her and she holds him. He does not do talking. Because of explosion two weeks. He said words. Water, bird, ball, Mama, Dada, my name. Now nothing. He just stares at us.

Our house explode and glass shatter. I scream and thought we all dead. E. had blood on his head and I was sure he dead like our neighbor who bleed all over his own floor. He still holds on to his head. All was twisted crazy mess but our house is made of iron and brick and cement and it stand fine. We thank Allah and give 2 goats to the poor. We are happy to stay alive. I have to believe and be happy Allah protect us. I am happy to breathe.

If we have no belief we have nothing.

I receive some emails and I reply soon.

Bye for now. Pray for peace.

Blue Sky

To: Blue Sky
From: Cassie
Subject: hi again from USA

Dear Blue Sky,

I just read your new blog post. Your life is very hard. I'm sorry about your house and your uncle and your brother and the dead body. That makes me sick too. I've never seen a dead body before. Is there any news about your uncle? I am most sad for your friend's family. No one should die at nine years old. Jack is almost nine.

I want everything to be like it was before this war too. My mother's convinced that Sef is going to die in Iraq. I can't believe that. The thing is, Sef is the one I am closest to in my family. Now he's not here, and everything's messed up, and I'm mad about everything. I know I shouldn't say this to you, but I feel like I can tell you things. I know you're mad about things too.

Sef wouldn't hurt anyone except in self-defense. He was always the one protecting us. He always wanted to make things right, that's what he's like. He doesn't think he is better than Iraqi people or anyone.

Please tell me more about your life, your friends, school, and family. I hope everything gets better soon and you are safe.

Bye,

Cassie

It turned out two hundred and fifteen people had been killed and more hurt in Sadr City, but Sef wasn't one of them. We received an email from him the next day. He wasn't even in Baghdad at the time of the attack.

To: Mom
From: Sef
Subject: Happy Thanksgiving!

Hi everyone,

Hope you had a Happy Thanksgiving! Sorry I didn't write sooner. We didn't have access to a computer because we were on a mission in the desert. They thought all these weapons and ammo were hidden there and the terrorists were bringing them into the city. We did a sweep and found some stuff. I don't want to say too much because I don't know who reads these emails, but don't worry. I'm fine. Except for the sand, which gets everywhere—my eyes, ears, mouth, nose—and it stings. Can you send a couple of sweatshirts, like the Pats one? Thank you for the package! It made my day.

The cookies were gone in seconds. The guys loved them, esp. Hurricane. He ate at least half.

You probably heard about the bombing yesterday. I'm sure you were worried, Mom. You probably heard about it before we did. Believe it or not, I heard it on the news. Don't worry, I'm OK!! The guys watch a lot of TV. We saw reruns of the 1986 Sox! Everyone had a good laugh. Go, Buck! Hurricane played *The Champ* for us. I'm not kidding, he CRIED. He's about the size of a house, and he cried.

I'm trying to remember all the things I wanted to tell you. The sunrise is sure beautiful in the desert. That's something I never would have guessed. I have a lot of time for thinking out here. If I think too much, I'll probably turn into one of those people who look like they're a million years old. One thing I know is it's hard to tell who the bad guys are. A few Iraqis still think Americans are good people. But to tell you the truth, I can't tell who's winning this war. Unless you're in the Green Zone. Then you think you're winning because it's so heavily guarded. They call it the Bubble too. It used to be where Hussein had his palaces. Now it's our government headquarters. They have swimming pools and bars—a little slice of heaven in all the hell. Not sure why they call it the Green Zone when it's mostly concrete and barbed wire.

I miss you guys a ton. Our whole troop prays before we go out. I wanna pray for everyone, but I don't really know what to say. It's easier with them than by myself. So far, so good with the brigade. Just Cali was sick from the water or something for a couple days, but he's better. I feel pretty safe with these guys watching my back. All in all, it's harder than anything I've done. Don't even ask about taking showers, Mom.

We have it so good at home. Don't forget that. THANKS again for the package!

I have to go because others are waiting for the computer.

Love,

Sef

CHAPTER 20

THREE-LEGGED DOG

WE READ SEF'S email together over and over. Mom clapped her hands and kissed Dad and Jack. Dad kept shaking his head. "We need to let him know we're winning."

"What?" Mom asked.

"Wouldn't he know if we were?" I said. "He's there."

"He should know," Dad said.

"Don't argue, please. He's fine, that's all that matters," Mom said. "He sounds just like himself."

"Who'd you think he was going to sound like?" Dad smiled.

"We're going out to eat as soon as Van gets home," Mom said.

We went to Layla's, where they made faces on Jack's pizza with tomatoes and pepperoni. On the way there, Mom rambled, "He sounded good, didn't he? Imagine Sef in the desert. I want to meet Hurricane, don't you?"

Dad said, "Why doesn't he know who's winning?"

"Of course we're winning. We're America," Mom said. "Bush said we were winning. He said that we're absolutely winning."

Van sighed. "I really wanted to go to Finn's practice tonight."

"Did you read Sef's email?" I asked.

"Yeah."

"Well, aren't you glad he's fine?" I tried to find her eyes, but her long hair hung like a shield over her face.

"Of course he's fine."

"Weren't you worried?"

She flung her hair back. Her dark eyes outlined in black pencil and heavy mascara were fierce. She bit her lip and said, "Nothing can happen to Sef." Then she turned to the window and went *tap tap tap* on the glass with her fingers.

When we pulled into the parking lot, she asked, "How long is this going to take? Finn's band is practicing."

"What's the name of his band again?" Dad asked.

"Solar Train."

Dad nodded slowly. "What does that mean exactly?"

"Does it have to mean something?" Van asked.

"Well, what kind of music is it?"

"It's rock, but it's not hard rock. It sounds really good."

"Finn's the main singer?"

"And songwriter."

"And he doesn't know any Sinatra?" Dad asked.

Van rolled her eyes.

Mom smiled. "Think they're going to be rich and famous soon?"

"They have a good chance," Van said.

Mom nudged Dad.

"I saw that," Van said.

"He'll probably be a millionaire, and we'll still be sitting here eating pizza at Layla's," Dad said.

"Not me," Van said.

"I want to stay here forever and ever," Jack said.

We ordered a sausage and eggplant pizza, and Van ordered a Caesar salad. Mom uncorked a bottle of wine from a paper bag and poured paper cups for her and Dad.

"Pow, pow, pow!" Jack played with his combat soldiers, hiding them behind the napkin holder.

"Don't shoot me," Dad said.

"When Sef was little, he used to play with those same soldiers all the time." Mom kept her eyes on the plastic soldiers. "When he was five, he told me he was going to be a soldier. I said, 'No you're not!' and he said, 'Yes I am.'"

"Guess he was right." Dad drank his wine.

"Thanks," Mom said.

The waitress slid our pizza and salad across the table. Van picked at the lettuce, glancing at the cell on her lap every few minutes. Mom held her folded slice in front of her. "You're not going anywhere until you have some pizza, Van. I mean it. Believe me, I know all about dieting."

"Take it from the beauty queen," Dad said.

"Don't ruin the night, Joe."

Van took a small slice, slid the cheese off, and took a bite. The rest of us stuffed our faces like we were trying to fill ourselves as fast as we could. Trying to fill the hole inside of us.

The waitress asked if everything was all right. Mom smiled and nodded. "Perfect."

I wanted to wipe that phony smile off her face. I wanted her to know there were things about Sef that I knew and she didn't. I asked, "Do you remember when Sef first started going to the gun club?" I looked at Jack's green plastic soldiers.

"What about it?" Mom frowned.

"Do you remember when he shot that three-legged dog?"

"What are you talking about?" she said.

Dad let out a deep breath.

"At the gun club when he was twelve or something."

"Is that true? He shot a dog, and you didn't tell me?" Mom asked.

Dad kept chewing.

"I thought he was practicing on targets," Mom insisted.

Dad put down his pizza and fired a look at me. "The dog tried to bite someone. They had to put him down. He probably had rabies."

"*Sef* had to shoot him?" she said. "You know how I feel about guns."

"It was six years ago. Don't make a big deal about this now." He wiped his mouth and took a long drink.

"Sef would never kill anything on purpose." Van put down her fork. Her face was white. "Is it true, Dad? I think I'm going to be sick." She ran into the bathroom.

"How did you know?" Mom asked me.

"Sef told me," I said.

"What else don't I know? What else haven't you told me?" She drew sharp breaths, in and out, in and out.

Jack stuffed another slice into his mouth.

"Cass, why are you bringing this up now?" Dad asked.

I thought of Sef watching the sunrise in the desert. I saw his face, but it wasn't laughing. It was older and gray. I turned to Dad. "Because it's the truth," I said.

PURPLE HEART

"JACK?" I CALLED. A rectangle of light fell through the window on the rug where Jack should have been. He wasn't in the kitchen or the dining room either, and I was supposed to be watching him. I ran back upstairs, even though I knew I would have heard him if he'd gone upstairs. All the rooms were empty. I checked the closets and under the beds, calling his name over and over.

"Come out if you're hiding, Jack. Please come out."

Except for my breath going in and out too fast, it was quiet. Something was wrong. I headed outside to the chestnut tree, running.

I started around the loop of our street, but there was no sign of Jack. He couldn't have gotten that far.

I sprinted back up toward our house. Just as I was about to cut through the Adamses' backyard, I saw him slumped over on the curb across the street with his head between his legs. He was shaking, but he wasn't crying. He wasn't making a sound.

"Jack!" I called.

Blood was dripping from his nose, and the front of his camouflage shirt was stained dark red. The side of his face was grayish blue where a bruise was slowly forming.

"What happened, Jack? Are you okay?" I sat down on the curb and put my arms around him. "It was Ben, wasn't it?"

He shook his head, pushed me away, and buried his face in his lap.

"You can tell me, Jack."

He lifted his head and wiped his nose with the back of his hand.

"Come on, let's go." I helped him up, my arm around his shoulders as we walked. "Who hurt you?"

He rolled his head in a circle.

I looked up at the big gray sky. "Was it stupid Ben?"

His eyes darted toward the Adamses' house. He frowned and shook his head again.

"You can tell me. He's not going to hurt you again. You shouldn't have gone out without me. You should have told me."

We went inside our house, and Jack sat on the couch. I told him, "Stay there, Jack. I'm going to clean you up."

First I wet some kitchen cloths and then I got the bacitracin and Band-Aids. If Ben did this, I was going to beat him to a pulp. I started wiping gently around Jack's swollen nose and beaten cheek. I could tell it was hurting him, but Jack didn't make a sound. His chest was going in and out as he breathed through his nose and pinched his mouth tight.

"You're so brave, Jack. You deserve a Purple Heart. Do you know what that is?"

He shook his head.

"It's a heart on a ribbon for our military wounded in battle. You're going to get a Purple Heart. Tell me where it hurts."

He pointed to his eye and nose.

"Does it hurt anywhere else?"

He spread his hand over the center of his chest.

"That hurts? Let me see." I lifted his shirt. There wasn't any mark. "Are you going to tell me what happened?"

He shook his head.

"Did you stop talking or something?"

He nodded.

"Really?"

He nodded again.

"Oh, great. Wait until Mom gets home."

Through the window I saw Mrs. Henderson walking her pug, Sid. I ran out and scratched him behind the ears. I asked her if she'd noticed anything unusual in the last hour. She hadn't. When I told her that Jack had been beaten up, she gasped and said, "It must have been someone outside the neighborhood."

I knocked on a few doors on our street to see if anyone knew anything. But no one did. They shook their heads and said they were sorry. I didn't want anyone feeling sorry for us. I wanted Jack to talk again, and I was going to make sure he did.

Of course Mom cried and cried when she saw Jack and held him on the couch, rocking him for a long time. She said she was going to call the police.

"What are they going to do?" Dad asked. "Start an investigation because a kid got a bloody nose? I don't want them here."

"Besides, he's not talking," I said.

"What do you mean he's not talking?" Mom said.

"Jack stopped talking."

"Say something," Mom said. "Please, baby, say something. Tell me who did this."

"He can talk," Dad said. "Go ahead, Jack, say something."

Jack just stared at the ceiling.

"Go ahead, you can do it," Mom told him.

He shook his head slightly.

"Oh, sweet Jesus," Dad said.

CHAPTER 22

WALKING INTO WALLS

I WOKE IN the dark. There was a loud bang and then the sound of shattering glass downstairs. I thought it was whoever beat up Jack. I jumped out of bed.

Dad said, "What's the matter with you, Van?"

"Nothing."

"Something is. What have you been doing?"

"Nothing."

"Are you drunk?"

"No."

"Were you drinking?"

"No." She giggled.

"What's so funny?"

"Nothing, I'm just really tired."

"Where were you?"

"Finn's."

"Go upstairs. We'll talk about it in the morning."

Van stumbled into our room, unzipped her high black boots, and let them clunk to the floor. Then she got into bed in her clothes and pulled the covers over her head. Van, who had always done everything right, was high on something again and walking into walls and tables and then hiding in the dark. We were all hiding from each other.

I took my blue stone from under my pillow. It smelled like salt. I waited for a sign that Sef was close by. But there was nothing. I stared at Van sleeping. I had told Sef I'd keep an eye on her, and I hadn't.

I woke in the middle of the night and tiptoed down the hallway to the bathroom. Jack was patting Van's back as she knelt beside the toilet.

The next morning everything outside was covered in white. The lamp on the end table in the living room was gone. Van was standing in sweats and a T-shirt in front of the mirror in the bathroom holding her toothbrush like a cigarette. Her dark eyes were half closed, and her head was tilted back so her wet hair fell straight down her back. She rocked back slightly, her free hand gripping on to the white porcelain edge of the sink. Her weight shifted from one leg to the other.

"Thanks for getting up last night when I was sick," she said in a small voice.

Jack's face gleamed. He held out the purple heart I'd cut from cardboard and tied with a purple ribbon the night before. When I gave it to him, I said, "Because you're so brave. Like Sef." Now he wanted to give his purple heart to Van.

Her eyes lifted a little. But there was no light in there. Where did it go? I took a step back. Jack lifted the purple heart closer to Van.

"Van," I said, "Jack has something for you."

She dropped her toothbrush into the sink and spun around, those lightless eyes searching us. "What?"

"Actually, you can't give it to someone else, Jack," I said, pulling him away from Van. "It's yours."

The air buzzed as Van started to blow her hair dry, cutting us off.

"Van?" I said.

"Van?"

Buzzzzz.

"Just wanted you to know, if you ever want to talk, you can talk to me," I said to her.

CHAPTER 23

THE KISS

THE MAIL FROM Saturday was still in our mailbox. There was a postcard for Jack of some famous building in Kuwait. It read, *Hey Jack, Hope you are taking care of everything there for me. Miss you, buddy. Love, Sef.*

I waved the postcard in front of Mom and Jack at the kitchen table. She clutched it to her, then read it out loud. Jack grabbed the card and tore out of his seat. He put on his coat and ran outside with it. Mom and I watched through the kitchen window as he raced through the snow to the chestnut tree, slicing the air with his postcard.

When I went outside, Jack was standing under the chestnut tree, staring at the postcard.

"Ask me to read it, Jack," I said, "and I'll read it to you."

He didn't say anything.

"Blue Sky's brother stopped talking too. You're going to talk to me, Jack. Soon, okay? Because I miss you."

He rested his head against the bark.

"I know you can hear me, Jack."

Inside, Mom was asleep on the couch. The TV was blasting. I thought of Blue Sky without electricity. How could she have so much hope when her world was falling apart around her? I wanted to be strong like that. I wanted to believe that things would get better. I decided right then that I really was going to make things better. I'd already told myself that I was going to be good, but I swore now that somehow I was going to reach Mom. I was going to find out what happened to Jack. And I was going to talk to Van.

I started collecting dirty plates, scraps of hot dog and dough-nuts, wineglasses, and coffee cups around the house and stacked them in the sink. I filled the sink with soap and water and washed everything. I cleaned the kitchen counter and dragged a cloth over the floor. I stuffed all the dirty clothes into the washing ma-chine, dumped in some soap, and turned it on.

I picked up around the sofa where Mom had fallen asleep. Sef's high school photo was on the cushion beside her. He had on a flannel shirt, and his brown hair fell over his forehead. His bluish green sea eyes were looking at me. In that second, I imag-ined his eyes were my eyes, his hair was my hair, his smile was my smile, and I was the one Mom missed.

I put my face close to hers. Her breath was warm, and her mouth was open. She was so pretty, even with the lines around the corners of her eyes and mouth. I wanted to tell her that it was going to be all right. I wanted to make things right again. I wanted to kiss her just as I'd seen her kiss Sef's picture. I leaned closer, and Mom stirred and shifted away. I stepped back and ran upstairs.

The shades were still drawn in Mom and Dad's room. Mom's bottles of cream and powder, blush, eyeliner and mascara were spread over her makeup table. Her clothes covered the chaise lounge. I fingered her creamy-colored silk shirts, her wool skirts, cashmere sweaters, light peach nylons as if I was going to find something that would tell me who she was.

I walked slowly down the hallway. I could see Jack's toys and puzzles on the floor of his room. I hadn't been in there for weeks. On his Thomas the Tank Engine night table were Dad's pens, gum wrappers, and change. His work pants were draped over the end of Jack's bed. I wondered how long Dad had been sleeping in there. My chest tightened. Everything was wrong.

I picked up a card from the comforter. It had a picture of a flock of ducks lifting off a pond, flying toward the blue sky ahead—an anniversary card with some gushy love poem written inside it. Their anniversary was over two weeks away. I let the card fall through my fingers to the ground. Dad really loved her. And despite everything, he wanted her to love him. I wanted her to love me too.

When I came back down, Mom was curled up on the couch. She opened her arms, and Jack slid inside. He wasn't talking, and he was her baby again. They were looking at the postcard from Sef.

I said, "I'm going to Kim's now, Mom."

She shifted closer to Jack and smiled blankly. "Okay."

I took off, breathing in the cold sharp air and breathing out puffs of white.

CHAPTER 24

JESUS STUFF

KIM WAS WATCHING for me in the lobby of her apartment building. She came clonking down the front walkway in her suede clogs and tight jeans, the ones with peace signs on the back pockets. Snowflakes clung to her hair.

"You're totally insane." She laughed at me.

A pickup truck drove in front of the apartment building. It was fixed with plywood signs along the sides painted in red capital letters: JESUS IS MY FRIEND, JESUS IS THE ANSWER, and JESUS IS THE REASON FOR THE SEASON.

"I'm insane?" I asked. "Who's that?"

"The one and only Jesus," Kim answered. "He lives in the middle building. Freak is his middle name. Supposedly he fell off his ladder one day, and when he woke up, he thought he was Jesus Christ. My mom says he's too lazy to work, so he pretends he's Jesus. Don thinks he's pretty fantastic. I think he's a creep."

A thin man with long straggly brown hair, wearing an oversized coat, jeans, and work boots, got out with a cup of Dunkin' Donuts coffee.

"Who would have guessed Jesus liked Dunkin' Donuts so much?" Kim rolled her eyes.

Inside his truck, Dunkin' Donuts cups, half-eaten doughnuts, napkins, flyers, and pamphlets covered the dashboard, and a worn-out Bible pressed up against the window. He waved and walked slowly toward us, stopping in front of me. He said slowly, "Something very difficult is going on with you." His eyes were soft and brown, prying into mine. They brightened. "It's your family. I can see it. You can tell me. I'm here to help."

He handed me his card. It said *Jesus at your service* above his phone number. Behind us, the wind rattled the plywood sign on his pickup, shaking the red words HE WILL COME AGAIN.

"Thanks," I said to him as Kim dragged me toward the door.

Waiting for the elevator, Kim said, "Don't worry. He says that to everyone. It's always 'the family.'"

We got off on the third floor and walked down the mustard-carpeted hallway. Kim's mother was on the couch in a white bathrobe, a book in one hand and a cigarette in the other. She was blowing loops of smoke around their living room. She lifted her masked face to us. Wet curls hung to her shoulders.

"Oh, hi. Hope you don't mind, I'm doing a peel before work."

I said, "My mom does them too."

"Doesn't seem to do any good for this old prune face, but I'm still trying."

"Cassie, Hannah, my mom. Cassie just got to meet Jesus downstairs."

"Lucky you. Did he give you a card?"

I held it up.

"Well, I'd rather live next to him than some child molester," she said.

"How do you know he's not a child molester?" Kim asked.

"Don't even say it." Her mother sucked in her breath.

After her mother went in to get ready for work, Kim and I started the poster. We wrote in red and green capital letters: CHRISTMAS DONATIONS FOR TROOPS FIGHTING IN IRAQ. On either side, I wrote in smaller letters: "Support Our Troops!"

"So what does this Jesus guy do, anyway?"

"I dunno. Prays, I guess."

"Have you ever called him?"

"No way. Please tell me you're not going to call him."

I shook my head. It wasn't like Jesus could bring Sef home. "Do you believe in heaven?"

"Sorta, I guess. Like I believe in magic. It feels sort of like believing in the Wizard of Oz."

"Well, I could use a little magic to make Jack start talking again," I said. "He stopped yesterday."

"What's up with that?"

"I don't know. He got beat up and stopped talking. I bet it was Ben Adams, the kid next door who's always picking on him. Kristen Adams's stupid little brother. But I don't know for sure because Jack won't say anything. I'm going to find out, though."

"I'll help. Was it bad?"

"Bloody nose, bruised cheek, broken heart," I said with a little smile.

"Poor kiddo."

"You know what's weird? Blue Sky's brother stopped talking

too. After their house was bombed. He's only two, but it's weird how we have these things in common. Even though I live here and she lives there. I feel like I can tell her things, and I don't really know her." I looked up. My cheeks were warm. "It's like that with you too. I mean, I can tell you things."

"Thanks," she said. "Except that I kind of wish *my* brother would stop talking. He thinks I talk a lot. He never shuts up."

After a while coloring in the block letters, Kim asked, "Think anyone's going to donate anything?"

"Sure. Rob said he would. Mr. Giraldi will."

"You like Rob, don't you?"

"How'd you know?"

"Your eyes tell everything." She smiled. "What about your friends—will they donate?"

"My so-called friends? Actually, I still miss Sonia sometimes."

"I know."

"It's weird not talking to her anymore. We used to be so close. Then she got busy with other stuff, and we ended up going in different directions. Our parents sort of got in this thing, too."

"Thing?"

"Yeah. It's complicated."

Kim waited, but didn't press me. She said, "Well, people change, right? Not always how you want them to."

Kim put on a Prince CD and danced. I used to dance with Sonia sometimes. Now I danced with Kim as I colored in the last letters. It felt good. She didn't judge. She wasn't watching me. She was busy shaking her own hips.

When we finished the sign, Kim showed me some video clips on her computer. One was of some troops in Iraq. They surrounded a statue of Saddam Hussein and started pulling it down with ropes. It toppled over. I remembered watching it on TV with Sef when the war first started. We had cheered afterward.

"Look," Kim said, pointing. "See the US military vehicle? Almost all American soldiers."

One of them draped an American flag over Saddam's face. Then the clip ended.

"Weird," I said. "I thought the Iraqis pulled it down."

"Our government wanted you to think that."

"Why?"

"So it looks like the Iraqis support our war. Like we're all in it together and doing something fantastic."

"That's pretty dumb," I said. "Kind of like that Wizard of Oz Jesus stuff."

"Yeah."

Did Sef know about this? Why did it feel like I was always getting tricked because adults said one thing and did another? Like *I* was supposed to figure out what was right and what wasn't all the time.

CHAPTER 25

TOUCHDOWN

IT WAS STILL snowing when we left, and Kim's mother insisted Don give me a ride home. Kim and I slid into his small black pickup. As we drove down Main Street, we saw Rob and Jesse and a few other guys throwing a football around in the town park. Kim elbowed me. Rob ran to catch the ball and slid on the white grass near us.

"That looks fun," I said.

"Fun?" she said.

"You know those guys, right? I've seen them at the court," Don said. He unrolled his window. "Hey, want a game?"

Kim groaned.

"Cool," Rob yelled back, and waved at us to come over.

"I'm not playing. No way. Football is not my thing," Kim said.

"Come on, you could probably play if you stopped talking long enough," Don joked.

Kim and I were heading over to watch them when Sonia, Michaela, and Lisa came walking down the sidewalk from town. Lisa, petite with long brown curls of hair, waved.

"What are you guys doing here?" Michaela asked.

"Hi to you too, Michaela," Kim said.

Michaela frowned and turned to me. "Did Sonia tell you she's trying out for cheerleading?"

"Not unless she did it telepathically," I said.

"Well, she is."

"You ready to play over there or what?" Jesse called to us.

I grabbed Kim's hand and pulled her forward. "You're on my team."

"What? I'm not playing."

"Yes you are."

"I thought we were just going to cheer from the sidelines," Lisa said.

"Nice try," Rob said. "Come on!"

We divided up into teams. Sonia and Michaela were on Rob and Jesse's team. Kim and I were with Don and Brandon. Sonia and Michaela pushed Lisa toward our team. "Have fun," Michaela told her.

As he headed to his end of the field, Rob said to me, "Don't even think you're going to win."

"Oh, yeah?" I said.

"Two-hand touch, everybody," Rob said.

The first play Don intercepted the ball, lobbed it to me, and I ran it in to score. Kim squeezed me. "You rock, girl."

"Oh, brother." Sonia rolled her eyes at Michaela.

Lisa slapped me five.

"Lucky," Rob said. "Pure luck."

"Yeah?"

"Yeah."

"We'll see about that." The cold air felt good on my cheeks. I held my hands out and caught the tiny flakes in my palms.

"Is that Dave Swanson over there?" Kim asked.

He was standing on the edge of the park, watching us.

"Hey, Swanson, come on over and play," Rob said. "You're on our team."

"What's he doing here?" Sonia said. "I thought he'd be home playing video games."

"All right, let's play ball!" Don said.

The next time I got the ball, Dave Swanson ran up and grabbed me around the waist, knocking me over. I might not have gone down if I hadn't been so surprised. He lay on top of my legs.

"Can you let me go now?" I asked.

"Okay," he said.

Brandon, who was too big to do much more than block, pulled Dave up. "Don't do that," he said. "You're gonna hurt her. It's two-hand touch, not tackle, Swanson."

Lisa gave me a hand. "I think he likes you," she whispered.

"He's got a funny way of showing it," I said.

She smiled.

The next play Dave grabbed the ball going to Michaela, almost knocking her over, and ran with it.

"Wow, thanks a lot," she said.

Rob yelled after him, "Hey, Dave, she's on your team, but now that you have it, go for it!"

As Dave ran, I saw there was something about the way his arms and legs were going out to the side, fast and out of control, that reminded me of Jack, and I felt sorry for him for a minute. He seemed so lonely running down the field by himself.

The next play Don lunged for the ball and slipped in the mud. We laughed since we were all covered in mud too. Even Michaela had given up cleaning off her jeans. Every play she positioned herself next to Rob, waiting for him. Rob dodged around me, growling as he passed. I caught up and tagged him. "Hey, you weren't supposed to do that," he said.

"Just lucky, right?"

Sonia caught a pass, but she forgot to run, as if she were too surprised to find the ball in her hands. Then Brandon got an interception and scored. He did a little dance, waving his hands high and shaking his hips around and around. I was laughing so hard, I had to bend over to catch my breath.

"Oh, yeah!" Don said. "How about next touchdown wins?"

Jesse threw the ball to Rob, but he tripped on Michaela. The ball spun to the right, then landed smack in Dave's hands, and he took off down the field. I might have been able to catch him, but I let him go, and when he got into the end zone, Rob and Jesse piled on top of him to congratulate him, and everyone else piled on top of them.

"You're going out for the team next year, Swanson," Jesse said. "Do you hear me?"

"Swanson, Swanson!" they chanted.

"This is the best day of my life!" he yelled.

Then Kim did a snappy hip-hop number that ended in a slide across the snowy grass.

Lisa clapped. "Did you guys see that? How'd you learn to do that?"

"Videos and stuff."

"Will you show me?"

The sky started turning black, and we could barely see the lights in the center through the powdery white snow. The night seemed to seal in the day, closing it up, and I felt this sadness and longing that made me almost cry. I wished we could have stayed just like the way we were on the field. I felt like the game had put us all on the same ground. I took a step closer to Rob and felt Dave's eyes on us. He had a huge smile that reminded me of Jack again. I turned away. I didn't have any more room to take care of anyone.

I thought of Jack at home. Sometimes he waited for Sef by the front window, and I wondered if he was waiting for me now. I hadn't told Mom I was going anywhere after Kim's. I said I had to go and I'd see everyone tomorrow. I let Kim and Don know that I was going to run home.

"I have to go too," Rob said. "I'll run part of the way with you."

I was glad for the dark. The only one I'd ever run with was Sef. It was strange running with anyone else. When we were halfway down the field, I asked, "Are you protecting me from Dave or something?"

"Seems like you're pretty good at taking care of yourself." He glanced at me. "And you're not bad at football."

"Next time we'll make a bet."

"You were lucky."

"Whatever you have to tell yourself."

I watched a smile spread across his face in the dark. He stopped running. "I go this way. See you tomorrow."

Tiny flakes of snow were falling in my hair and face. I looked up at the white sky, and suddenly I wasn't sad anymore.

CHAPTER 26

WAR TACTICS

Blue Sky's Blog

December 10, 2006

Today we have exams. Many students do not arrive school on time because of the blockades. They were crying and afraid and had to start exams late. I am lucky I arrive on time.

I try to be strong but many times I shake at night. Remember my friend is Shiite. We stop visits for now. We are all Iraqis but now everyone has fear. There is Al Sadr with thousands behind him. He is a Shiite, son of a martyr who tries to reverse history. Sistani is no better. There are Iranian militias not in best interest for Iraq. My father say Iran is behind all. They play Iraq like an instrument. Our government is not strong. We need Iraqis who live here and understand our country. Not Iraqi exiled for years. It is complicated. Our boundaries are not protected. Terrorists run in.

Many Iraqi have no money. Their houses and shops are ruined and the price of kerosene, medicine, gas, drinking water, food is very high. No jobs are available. They make money looting, kidnapping, killing.

There is not news on my uncle. Nothing. We are upset and Mom cry and cry. And our beautiful city is gone. It is rubbles. It is also like losing someone close.

Sometime I wake and think everything is same as before the war but I only look out my window and see I am wrong. We can do nothing to stop it but watch as things grow worse.

My parents try to keep it from me but I hear the stories. American used chemical weapon in Fallujah. The story is people are burned to the bone. I saw pictures on the computer. I do not think about this much or I am very sick. I thank Allah to keep us alive.

Why is it some people has almost everything and they are not happy? Do I no before the war I am happy?

Blue Sky

To: Cassie
From: Sef
Subject: Re: Re: I'm here

Hi Cass,

I haven't had time to write. My patrol shifts are 12 hrs long, sometimes all night, guarding a police station. I'm soaking my feet now. It feels so good, I don't want to put on these boots again.

The days are so long. I swear a couple of the guys have gained weight here. Like Cali, now known as the fat surfer dude. There's a lot of sitting around. Sometimes we play this poker game, Texas Hold 'Em. I'm going broke.

Mark that skinny dude from Illinois gets a letter from his mother almost every day. We tease the hell out of him. His mom wanted him to go to college too. I feel bad for his mom, but I feel worse for the guys who are married and have kids. Tim has a tattoo of his three kids on his back. They're all under 5 and cute as hell.

It's crazy here. Almost everywhere you look, buildings and cars are blown up. When I first got off the plane, I smelled smoke. Now I'm so used to it I don't even notice.

One good thing is we passed out soccer balls, notebooks, and pens to some kids on the street. I even played a little soccer, which was great. Definitely the best thing that's happened here so far. The kids played in bare feet, and we played in our uniforms. The field was mostly dirt, and we used our boots for goalposts. I was so hot I was dying. Try running in one of these uniforms sometime!

I'm glad Jack's staying in my room—as long as he doesn't pee in my bed too much. That's cool about the Iraqi girl. What's she say?

Have to go, time's up. I'll write again when I can. Hope everyone's hanging in there. Miss you.

Love,

Sef

To: Sef

From: Cassie

Subject: Re: Re: Re: I'm here

Hey Sef,

Do you really stand for twelve hours straight? Sounds like torture. I love the picture of you driving the tank. You look tiny! Jack wouldn't stop looking at it. Seriously, I couldn't get back on the computer for about two hours! Luckily Mom printed a bunch of copies. Jack carries his around. He's still wearing camouflage every day, and Van's still being Van.

Kim showed me that video clip of the Saddam Hussein statue falling, the one we watched when the war started. Most of the troops there were Americans. It looks like they planned it all out. When I asked Dad, he said it was war tactics. They were psyching us up. But they're not supposed to trick us, are they? From now on, I'm going to try to find out the truth about things.

The Iraqi girl, Blue Sky, says we used chemical weapons in Fallujah—is that TRUE?

You know what? The other night when I was running, I thought you were close by. It was pretty cool. I miss you.

Love,

C

CHAPTER 27

THE TABLE

KIM AND I set up our donation table by the entrance to the cafeteria with the poster we made and the few boxes of energy bars Mom had given me. Kim had made a list of things the troops might need, including batteries, flashlights, trail mix, sunglasses, sunblock, Gatorade, razors, snacks, paper, pens, and wipes. A few of the teachers stopped by and said they'd bring something tomorrow. Michaela and her friend Meg stopped in front of the table. Michaela looked at Kim and then me and said, "Did your mom make you do this?"

"Do what?"

"Your donation table."

"No." My cheeks were hot.

"I was just wondering because it's so *crazy*." Michaela smirked. What had Sonia been telling her?

"What's your problem, Michaela?" Kim asked. "Jealous, by any chance?"

"Of *what*?" she asked. "Anyway, I don't have a problem. I think Cassie has the problem."

"Oh, yeah? What's that?" Kim asked.

"You're the one with, like, the biggest mouth in the school. Why don't you ask her?"

"*Like*, that's a very good question," Kim said.

Meg elbowed Michaela as Rob jogged up holding out a Replacements CD. "Good?" he asked.

"Great. He likes them." I held on to the CD. "Thank you."

His eyes held mine for that second.

Michaela squinted at Kim's lunch. "What's that?"

"Raw fish. Want to try some?" Kim held up an oily pink slab of fish.

"Yuck. That's disgusting."

Rob grabbed the fish and dangled it in front of Michaela. "It's good for you. It gives you protein—and courage. Try a little."

She shrieked and backed up, but she was smiling.

He swung it closer to her. "Watch out, or it might bite you!"

"Rob, stop it!" She swatted him, half laughing.

"Mmmm," Rob said, and opened his mouth and dropped it in. "Delicious!"

"I can't believe you did that. That is, like, so gross," Michaela said, flipping her hair over her shoulder. "You'd eat anything." She pushed him on the chest, and he pretended to fall back.

When they left, Kim said, "You should do something about that."

"This?" I held the CD out.

"No."

"Oh," I said. *About Rob.*

"What's the matter with Michaela, anyway?" Kim asked. "Why'd she say that about your mother?"

I could feel my chest thumping. I swallowed and started talking. I told her about our family and Sonia's family being friends and about my mother and Sonia's father flirting in our kitchen. About how Sonia stopped talking to me after that. About how Jack freaked Sonia out sometimes. I told her about all of it, and Big Mouth Kim listened. When I was done, she nodded and said, "Wow, that's a lot of stuff you're carrying around. A lot of weight on your shoulders, as my mom says. You okay?"

"Yeah, I'm okay."

"What about Sonia's dad? Isn't it just as much his fault?"

"Yeah, it is." I laughed. It felt good to say it. "Of course it is."

The bell rang, and we packed everything on the table into a cardboard box and took it to the school office to store until tomorrow. On the way to English, Kim said, "You should read the end of *The Giver*."

"I know what happens."

"What?" she asked.

"Jonas gets on his bike and rides out of the Community with the baby. Some people think they die, but——"

"You finished it!" Kim interrupted.

"No, but I read the last few pages. It made me want to take Jack and ride away from here."

"Except Jack's not a baby."

"Yeah, that's true," I said. "Do you think they die?"

"No way." She looked straight at me. "They find Christmas."

"That's what I'm going to do—find Christmas. I swear I'm going to make things better."

"Just like that?" She snapped her fingers.

"Yeah."

"Okay, Supergirl."

I laughed and puffed myself up until I really did feel bigger.

The next day at our table, Kim told me, "I was five when my mom and dad got divorced. They used to fight all the time," she said. "Not saying your parents need to get divorced. But I used to think it was all my fault, and it wasn't, of course. But there wasn't anything I could do to change them, that's for sure. They were just awful together. Parents are weird."

"I know for a fact that my dad loves my mom, so I have to try."

"You're right," Kim said. "My dad moved to California."

"Do you see him now?"

"A couple times a year. I'm going to see him at Christmas and this summer. It's fine. My mother's really my best friend."

"Really? I can't imagine that."

Dave Swanson came over with a box of Oreos. He slid them across the table and left.

"Thank you," we called after him.

"Won't these get crushed traveling six thousand miles?" Kim said. "Maybe we should eat them. I love Oreos."

"I do too, but I'd feel too guilty." I glanced over where Dave was sitting. "Should we invite him over to sit with us sometime?"

"He does seem lonely, doesn't he? And he was pretty funny playing football."

"Yeah. He asked me to the Spring Dance last year, you know."

"I take it you said no."

"He's barely looked at me since. Until he tackled me on Sunday."

"That was a nice way of getting your attention again," Kim said. "I think we should wait to ask him to sit with us. You don't want to mislead him. And you have enough on your plate."

"You're right." I was relieved. "Did you go to the dance?"

"No, even though I *can* dance."

An eighth-grader plunked a package of lighters on the table. A few of the teachers had brought in packages of bars and trail mix, notebooks, pens, and batteries. Mr. Giraldi offered us a couple of videotapes with sports bloopers. Some kids gave us packages of candy and gum. One even donated a digital camera. Miss Pat contributed some school sweatshirts.

"Thanks for doing this with me, Kim," I said.

"Anything for you, Supergirl," she said. "By the way, what *are* you going to do?"

"Start by giving my mom a normal pill."

We were cracking up as Rob jogged by and waved. I sucked in my breath.

Kim nudged me. "I think he likes you. Or maybe he likes Supergirl."

"Actually, I think he likes everyone, but I don't care. I'll be right back, okay?" I didn't wait. I sprinted down the hallway. I *was* going to do something.

I ran past Sonia and was surprised to feel this hurt open inside of me. On Sunday she had smiled and we had fun. Now she was like Mom—in a Deep Freeze again. I realized that it wasn't just that I missed Sonia—it was that something was missing. In the last year, I'd become the one who tried hard. I wanted her to try, too. I wanted her to like me for me, not for my clothes and hair and stuff.

I could see Rob's flannel shirt up ahead. My head felt light. I was suddenly right behind him. Jesse elbowed him, and he turned around.

"Hey." He looked at me. Jesse walked a little ahead, then stopped to watch us.

"I have to go back"—I pointed to the cafeteria—"but I just wanted to tell you that I can go to Fresh if you can. Since you asked before."

"We don't have practice Friday afternoon."

Jesse shoved Brandon in our direction. Brandon tripped and his books scattered across the floor. Rob grinned. "Okay?"

"Okay, Friday." I waved a little and turned around and almost ran over Sonia. I smiled at her and then sprinted back to help Kim pack up our table.

SUPERGIRL

I WALKED THROUGH the kitchen, dining room, and living room. Everything was exactly the way I'd left it this morning, but I felt bigger somehow. Because they needed me. And being called Supergirl really did make me stronger. And I was going to Fresh on Friday with Rob. Because I asked him. I breathed in deep, holding on to this. I decided to do something, and I did it. I was in charge of my life. I could change things. I realized that was what Sef had always known.

Jack was sitting on the couch in the spot where Mom usually sat. He stared at the blank TV screen.

"Come on, Jack, let's make some Christmas decorations. Those salt dough ones. You get the flour and salt out. I'll Google the recipe."

When I returned, Jack was sitting at the table with the silver mixing bowl on his head. I shouted, "Supergirl is here!"

Jack smiled at me.

"That's right. You heard me—Supergirl! I can leap onto the highest counters." I jumped onto the counter under the baking cabinet to get the salt and flour. I held them high, spread my arms, and flew down. I ran to the table and set them in front of Jack. "I'm faster than a speeding bullet."

A noise cracked between his lips. He clapped his hands over his mouth.

I dashed back and forth again. "The one and only Supergirl!"

A rolling laugh exploded out of Jack's mouth as if it had been waiting there for a long, long time. I felt my insides swell, and my heart nearly exploded. I waved my arms and leapt up and ran back and forth in the kitchen. "I'm Supergirl, and you're going to start talking and tell me what happened. That's what any good marine would do."

I waited. "You'll be happy again, Jack. Are you happy?"

Nothing.

"You can tell me later. For now, let's mix this dough up."

We mixed the flour and salt, and then added water. We kneaded and rolled out the dough on the floury table. We cut out angels, stockings, and Santas, and rolled candy canes and wreaths until we heard Mom's car pull into the garage. Her door slammed, and next thing, she was in the kitchen with the remote in hand.

"Hi," she said as she clicked on the TV. "What do we have here?"

"Christmas decorations," I said. "Mom, when are we going to get a tree?"

"Oh, we have plenty of time, don't worry. We'll get a tree," she said.

"When?"

"Closer to Christmas." She squinted at me. "Do you have to wear that old sweartshirt every day?"

I tucked the ends of the sleeves, which were beginning to fray, into my palms. "It's Sef's."

"It doesn't look like Sef's anymore. His clothes were clean. I want you to wash that, do you understand?"

I didn't answer.

Mom started clanging down the pots and pans.

The man on CNN said, "—for the first time yesterday that the United States is not winning the war in Iraq and said he plans to expand the overall size of the US armed forces to meet the challenges of a long-term global struggle against terrorists."

Click, click went the remote control, the volume going higher.

"Asked in an interview with *Post* reporters if the US is winning in Iraq, President Bush said, 'You know, I think an interesting construct that General Pace uses is, *We're not winning, we're not losing.*'"

Mom slammed the remote down. "Do you remember right before the election, you said, 'Absolutely, we're winning'—do you remember that, Mr. President? I do! Because we have to win this stupid war!" She marched out of the kitchen.

"I don't know if we were ever winning," I said to Jack. "But don't tell Mom. She doesn't want to know."

Jack stared back at me.

"Don't forget I'm Supergirl and you're going to start talking. When you talk, you can do whatever you want. You can be anyone you want!"

His eyes widened.

"What about when Sef calls again?" I said. "You'll want to

talk to him, right? Give him the update. He'll probably call on Christmas."

His mouth opened.

We heard Mom padding down the stairs. I leaned toward him. "And don't you want to call us to supper again? I miss that. It's not the same when Mom does it. That was your job. Please talk again, okay? You're going to take charge, champ. I know it."

Jack stood straighter and breathed in deep. Then he pulled his toy soldiers out of his pocket and stuck them in the lump of salt dough.

Later that night I tried to find my hoodie. I looked through the piles of clothes in our room, in the blankets and sheets of my bed, the laundry basket in the bathroom. I checked Jack's and Sef's room, then ran to the laundry room. I could see it in there with all the clothes going around and around in the soapy water. Washing Sef away.

"Mom!" I yelled. "Why did you wash my hoodie?"

"Because it was disgusting," she said. "And it's not yours."

"It was good luck the way it was." I ran up to Sef's room and slammed the door. Jack watched me open each of Sef's drawers, throwing T-shirts and sweatshirts out of their neat piles. I smelled them all, then opened his closet and tore down the piles on the shelf. Mom must have washed everything in here.

I sat down on the floor and held my face in my hands with my eyes closed. When I opened them, Jack was standing there with a long-sleeved Baltimore Orioles T-shirt. Sef used to wear it running. It smelled of sweat and sweet spice. I held it to my face, then put it on. I would sleep in this one every night.

HAPPY

MOM WAS MAKING a special dinner. She was washing portobello mushrooms at the sink, wearing the leopard-spotted apron that Dad gave her. Her heart-attack-in-a-pan casserole with sausage and cream was sitting on the stove, ready to cook. On the counter were a bottle of wine, a baguette, and salad.

"Can you get the potatoes ready, Cassie? I'm going to put on my face. Dad's coming home early."

"Put on your face for supper?" I asked.

"It's our anniversary," she said.

I scrubbed six potatoes, the same number I always scrubbed, one for each person, including Sef. I felt Jack behind me, heard his feet shuffling softly in and then out of the kitchen. The phone rang. It was Kim, calling to tell me that her mom was donating shaving cream and chocolate to send to Iraq. When I hung up, all the cleaned potatoes were gone.

"Jack, what did you do with the potatoes?" I called.

Of course he didn't answer, and I couldn't find them

anywhere, so I took out six more potatoes from the ten-pound bag. I scoured the dark eyes behind each pocket of dirt on their skin, and Mom put them in the oven with the casserole. Her eyes were outlined in dark pencil, and her lips were cherry colored. She wore her high heels with her jeans and apron.

When Dad came home, he called out, "Smells good in here, honey," and gave Mom a dozen red roses.

"Let's have a glass of wine before dinner," she said. She popped the cork and poured two glasses. "Cassie, call everyone for supper, would you?"

I marched through the living room. "Jack, where are you? I know you're hiding in here somewhere."

He was sitting behind the couch. His hands were fists on either side of his head. The picture of all of us that Mom had taken the day Sef left for Iraq was propped up in his lap. Mom had blown it up and set it in a gold frame. Everyone was smiling except me, but Mom's eyes were red and puffy, and Van's eyes were wide, like she'd been blinded by the flash. I hadn't noticed before, but Sef seemed swallowed up in Dad's big leather chair.

It suddenly made me so mad that Sef seemed all alone. Even though we were standing close together, no one was actually touching. I picked up the framed photo. I wanted Sef back, and I wanted the old Jack back, the one in the photo. I dropped the photo hard on the ground, and the glass cracked into hundreds of tiny pieces. I stood over Jack.

"Supper, Jack!" I called. "Supper, Jack! Supper!"

A low gurgling sound rose from Jack's chest. He jumped up. His eyes, bright and hard, darted around the room. He ran to the kitchen, picked up a plate, and flung it like a Frisbee across the room. It smashed against the wall. Mom screamed. Jack started kicking and flinging whatever else he could reach, including the creamy sausage casserole. I got behind him and held his arms to his sides.

Dad stood behind me. "Okay, Cass? Need help?"

"I think I'm good."

Jack tried to free his arms. I pulled him down to the ground and tried to make a shell over him. He grunted and breathed hard. He wriggled his body over the floor, his arms and legs flailing in the air. Then he closed his eyes and started punching his own head, face, and chest.

"Stop, Jack," I begged. "Please, please stop." I wrapped my arms tighter around him from the back. The black rim of his glasses was cracked. He jerked around and threw his head back into my face. I pressed myself into his neck until I could feel him start to give in. "Shhh, Jack. It's okay, it's okay."

Slowly he stopped struggling and let his arms and legs go. Even when he was still, the house seemed to be rocking back and forth. Mom tried to take him in her arms, but Jack clung to me. Dad picked up broken plates and glasses and food and dropped it all in a garbage bag. I half carried, half dragged Jack back to the couch. He stuffed White Kitty in his shirt, and his eyes rolled back in his head like he was dead.

"So much for our anniversary dinner," Mom said, looking at the mess. "Looks like we'll try plan B. Layla's Pizza?"

"We'll have them deliver," Dad said.

Just before we sat down to eat, Mom called out, "For crissake, what's the matter with the toilet? It's all backed up. Where's Jack? Joe!"

Dad spread the toilet parts across the porch floor. From the kitchen we watched him pull six scrubbed potatoes out of the pipes. He held them up in the air, shaking his fists.

"Happy anniversary," Mom called to Dad. "Twenty years!"

Dad raised a potato to her. "Happy anniversary."

Mom laughed and drank her wine. Her lips were tinged red like her teeth. Dad started belting out, "Fly me to the moon. Let me sing among those stars—"

"Dad," Van groaned, "really, do you have to sing?"

We laughed and ate our pizza. I told Mom that Kim and I had set up a donation table to collect things for the troops.

"You did?"

I nodded.

"What can I do?"

"Nothing, unless you want to donate something. We're going to send the box at the end of next week so it gets there in time for Christmas."

"Thank you."

"For what?"

"For doing that." She smiled at me like she used to, and I knew that after all these days of it, the Deep Freeze was officially over. At least for now. Maybe Jack's silence had shown her how it felt when it happened to her.

"Mom?"

"Yes?"

I wanted to ask her why things were so messed up and why

people never seemed happy even when they had everything, but I couldn't remember the last time she had smiled at me like that. I said, "Oh, nothing."

Later when I was doing my homework in the kitchen, I heard Mom ask Dad, "It's been five days. What are we supposed to do about Jack?"

He turned the football game down. "It's not like we can make him talk," he said. "What can we do?"

"I don't know."

"What about the speech therapist at school?" Dad asked.

"You think he can make him talk? I doubt it. Jack's so stubborn."

Then Dad asked, "What about Van?"

"What about Van?"

"Well, she's getting into trouble with Finn. She was drinking the other night, remember?"

"Van's got a good head on her shoulders. She'll be fine," Mom said. "Honey, let's take one thing at a time."

Dad sighed. The TV volume went up, up, up.

It seemed to me that it was never one thing at a time. Things piled up and up and up until Mom couldn't stand it anymore and in her Mom way pulled everything crashing down like the Saddam Hussein statue.

After the toilet had been reassembled and Jack was in bed, Dad and I sat in the living room. Outside I could see the tops of the spindly dark branches of the trees against the sky.

"How's school going?" he asked.

"Pretty good."

"So, you're collecting things to send to Iraq." He popped a chocolate macaroon into his mouth.

"Yes."

"You're a good kid." He leaned back in his leather chair.

"Dad, what's up with Mom?"

His eyes closed, and his head dropped.

"The toilet overflowing was a nice anniversary present for you," I said.

He smiled. "I don't know what happened. She snapped on me."

"Everything seems so messed up"—I took a deep breath—"since Sef decided to leave."

"Yeah, I know." His eyes filled. He wiped underneath them with the back of his hand. "I miss that kid."

I'd never seen him cry before. I didn't want to. His heavy cheeks seemed to sag, and for the first time, I noticed little gray hairs near his temples.

"What are we going to do, Dad?"

"I don't know. We'll figure it out." He sighed. "Your mother and I are working it out, don't worry. It's not your fault."

"You're not going to move out or anything?" I tried to laugh, but it sounded more like choking.

"No, I'm not going anywhere. At the rate I'm going, I'll be too fat to go anywhere."

We laughed. I felt a sudden stab of relief.

"Everyone seems to think I look good fat." He sighed and

rubbed the top of my head. "Things will get better soon, kiddo."

"Promise?"

"Promise."

"Okay, thanks. Good night, Dad."

He went upstairs. Outside was dark and frozen. I sat there for a long time.

The next night, Mom's makeup lights were on. She was smoothing foundation over her face. She glanced in the mirror at me in the doorway, then rubbed blush along her cheekbones. The tiny gold cross around her neck swung toward me like a blade of sunlight. Dad had given it to her last Christmas. She hadn't worn it for so long, I thought this was a sign that things were going to be normal again. I wanted to reach for it and feel the cool, delicate gold slip through my fingers.

"Come in, Cassie," she said.

On the corner of the table was a photo of Sef as a baby. I picked it up. He was fat and bald and smiling. Mom leaned to the light and plucked out a gray hair with tweezers.

"I want you to do something for me, Cassie."

"What?"

"Don't worry about everything. Dad and I will take care of us. You don't need to." She squeezed my chin between her finger and thumb. "Will you do that?"

I nodded. "I will, but it still doesn't make it okay."

She turned back to the mirror. "I didn't say it was okay."

"Sonia hasn't talked to me at all. What am I supposed to tell her?"

Mom glanced at me. "Tell her it's nothing to do with you or her."

"Sounds easy." I sighed.

She breathed out. "No one said it was easy. But we're still going to be the family we always were."

CHAPTER 30

YOUR FAMILY IS BREAK

To: Blue Sky
From: Cassie
Subject: Re: hi again from USA

Dear Blue Sky,

I talked to my dad tonight. I've never seen him cry before. Have you ever seen your dad cry? It was awful. Something is going on with my mom. She was totally flirting with my friend Sonia's dad right before Sef left. I don't understand it. Of course it was Sonia's dad's fault too. She's so messed up. Everything is messed up and I'm trying to hold our family together. But Jack's not talking, just like your little brother, and Van is still drinking. Sometimes I think I'll wake up and Sef will be home and everything will be like it used to be.

I can't find any reporting that we used chemical weapons in Fallujah. I feel so sick writing and thinking about that.

How is your family? Is your brother talking? Any news about your uncle? I hope your electricity is on and you can write soon. I am going to try to be strong and hopeful like you.

Your friend,

Cassie

To: Cassie

From: Blue Sky

Subject: Re: Re: hi again from USA

Dear Cassie,

Electricity is off and on in small connection. Most off.

Try to honor your mother and father. No matter what they are your parents.

Later I try to write.

Blue Sky

To: Cassie

From: Blue Sky

Subject: Re: Re: Re: hi again from USA

Dear Cassie,

I respond to the email you send. Your mother flirt with another man? That can not happen here. Your family is break. It fix soon I believe. They want to break my family too. My father was English teacher but he lost job after war start, so he become interpreter for American military. Pay well and he like people and work. Now he has threat. They call on the phone and tell us to leave Iraq or else. He think America will help him. Not much time. We leave or stay. Iraq is everything for us. I am afraid for life. How to leave before we find Uncle???

My father check the morgue everyday and each time when he come back my mother cry for tiny hope he is alive. The terrorists do not care, they take whole families, mothers, and children. We phone the Red Cross and lawyers but we are the one in thousands so nothing happen. We hear if they beat person only that person is lucky. Lucky to have a beating! You are lucky Cassie. You walk outside and no one hurt you.

I have drowning attack like you call before. I wait for it and it sometime happen, sometime no. Sometime I dream to be stuck under bricks and cement. Not to move. But I believe and thank Allah and live. Writing make less panic for me. But I have a little time for my blog.

How is Van? She speak to you? She sick? Your family will fix again.

Some good news to end. My brother speak my name today! I was more happy than words for that. We celebrate and prepare special food. Your brother follow soon. I went to school today and was happy. Even to see my Geography teacher who is terrible mean.

Best regards,
Blue Sky

To: Blue Sky
From: Cassie
Subject: Re: Re: Re: Re: hi again from USA

Dear Blue Sky,

Why do they threaten your family? Who exactly and is it because your father worked for us? America has to help. And what do you mean, We leave or stay?

Your dream is scary. I have this dream sometimes where I am running but I never get anywhere. I go faster and faster, and when I wake up, I think I can't breathe. But I can. What do you do with all that panic stuff? When you can't breathe? Where does it go, I mean? Either I go running or I put my head down low and imagine that I'm running. Then I can breathe again.

Christmas is coming, and it seems like Sef's been gone forever. I am so worried he won't come back. I panicked the other night when I had a dream he blew up. I woke in the middle of the night and put my face out the window. Writing to you helps too. I start to sort everything out. I'm happy about your brother. I hope Jack is next. Sorry you have no news about your uncle. I am sorry for your mother and father.

Write again soon, please.

Your friend,
Cassie

CHAPTER 31

TODAY IS FRESH

ON FRIDAY AFTERNOON, the rain turned to sleet and then snow. We watched through the cafeteria window. "Maybe it will stop," I said to Kim. But part of me didn't want to go to Fresh. What if Jack threw a tantrum? Or worse. And what was I supposed to say to Rob, anyway? What if it ended up he didn't like me?

I picked up my sandwich and put it down. "Think I should cancel?"

"No way."

"What if he doesn't show?"

"I'm sure he'll show. But if he doesn't, then at least you know."

"Know what?"

"He's not worth it." She shrugged.

In English Mr. G asked if I was feeling all right. "I'll tell you Monday," I answered.

After school I went to Jack's class. Something was wrong with Jack. He wouldn't look at me. I glanced around the room for

163

Jack's teacher, Ms. Bennett, but she wasn't there. The Hillview Middle School language specialist walked toward me. If there was a substitute, I usually stayed with Jack until I knew he'd be fine.

"Ms. Bennett went home sick this morning," she explained. "I tried to get Jack to talk to me, but he refused. He had to sit there for most of the afternoon." She smiled and pointed to the chair in the corner of the room.

Jack was red. His arms and hands and face were red. Even his eyes were rimmed red.

I turned to take his hand. "Come on, kiddo. Today is Fresh."

His hips and shoulders wriggled upward and then his head seemed to pop like something had snapped inside of him. He ran out the door and down the hallway, his Diego backpack slapping his side. His glasses started to slip off, so he held them in place. He couldn't see without them. I could have gone faster, but I didn't want anyone to see me chasing Jack through school. Besides, he couldn't go that fast. He was bowlegged, and he waddled when he ran.

"Slow down!" someone yelled. A few kids laughed and jumped out of the way. I thought he would stop, but he ran out the front door, down the main entrance, toward the parking lot. He looked around wildly.

There was a group of kids across the parking lot. Someone had on camouflage pants. Jack darted in the direction of the camouflage.

"Jack!" I yelled. "Wait for me!" That's when I finally started running. I was the runner, and I had let him go.

The front walkway had been shoveled and sanded, but there were patches of ice in the parking lot that were newly frozen. Jack hadn't zipped his coat, so it flapped like wings, and he slipped, almost flying through the air. I saw the red Volkswagen coming the other way. The tires screeched, and it skidded, sliding across the ice toward Jack. I heard someone say, "Oh, my God!" Another person screamed. I waited for a big thudding sound. But there was only silence. The car had stopped inches in front of Jack. He stood, staring into the front window of the Volkswagen.

I couldn't move. I heard people talking.

"Wow, that was close."

"Who is that?"

"It's that kid who thinks he's a soldier."

"The special-needs kid."

"That was crazy. Is he okay?"

"I think so. Who is he, anyway?"

It's Jack, I thought. *Just Jack*. He stood there, searching the crowd of people who had gathered around the car.

Rob broke out of a group of friends and ran to me. He grabbed my hand. His hand was warm as he pulled me out of my frozen place toward Jack.

"Jack!" I yelled. "Here I am. Jack!"

Jack took a step back from the car and collapsed. There was more screaming. I ran in front of Rob. Jack's eyes were closed, but there wasn't a scratch on him. I lifted his head into my lap and told him to look at me. He did. His eyes were full of tears.

Our gym teacher, Mr. Mac, was kneeling beside us. "I'm so sorry. I didn't see him. I don't think I hit him. I don't think I touched him at all."

"It wasn't your fault," I said. "He's okay."

Ahead of us, the buses were pulling away from the school.

"Let me take you home," he said. "Can I lift him?"

"Yes, he's fine. Just shell-shocked." I smiled at Jack.

Mr. Mac scooped Jack up and laid him on the backseat. I slid in beside him. Rob waved to us as we pulled out of the school parking lot. My chest was heavy.

On Monday Rob found me by my locker. "Is Jack okay?"

"He's fine." I looked up at him. He was standing so close, I could smell a soapy cotton smell. I felt myself sway backward. I had to lean on my locker. "Sorry about that."

"You definitely don't need to apologize to me. Things happen," he said. "We'll go to Fresh another time. But my cousins are staying with us for a couple of weeks, so my mom says I can't plan anything until after Christmas. We could do it right after that. Can I have your email or something? I wanted to check in with you over the weekend, but I didn't have it."

"Okay." I must have looked disappointed. I turned and stared into my locker, trying to remember what I was supposed to get.

He said, "Everything all right, Cass?"

"Yes."

He waited. Kids running by slowed to watch us. I didn't even look to see if one of them was Sonia.

I looked into his eyes and said, "It's been stressful at home." I couldn't believe I was telling him this.

He nodded.

"Since Sef left. The whole year, really."

"Yeah."

The bell rang.

"Now I made you late."

He shrugged. "So? I made you late."

I laughed.

"You could run. You're pretty fast," he said.

"Yeah, I am."

"You gonna race me sometime?" he asked slowly.

"I really don't want to beat you," I said.

"Uh-oh. That's a challenge if I ever heard one." He laughed. "Let's make that official."

I wrote down my email on a slip of paper.

Of course I told Kim right away. She squeezed my arm and said, "I'm not going to tell you I told you so."

"Promise?"

"Promise." She smiled big at me.

CHAPTER 32

WE WILL FLY
TO SUCCESS

AS WE GOT closer to Christmas, Mom and Dad were so polite with each other, it was weird. I thought of what Blue Sky said about honoring your parents no matter what, and I went back and forth, trying to understand them and then being mad. It was so quiet all the time with Van sleeping and Jack not talking.

At lunch, when I told Kim that I wasn't making any difference, she said, "You can't change anyone else, you know. Just yourself, Supergirl."

I laughed. "Well, I'm going to try. At least Jack."

"Like in *The Giver*?" she asked.

"Yeah."

"Okay, let's take Jack sledding," she said, "and we'll find Christmas."

On Saturday morning the sky shone blue. We put the toboggan in the back and crowded into the front of Don's pickup.

"Personally, I think you guys are crazy going sledding this early on Saturday morning. I can't believe I'm even up right now," Don said.

"Um, because I paid you five dollars last night?" Kim said.

"Oh, yeah." He smiled and glanced at me. "How's Sef holding up?"

"Pretty well. He says his feet get tired because the shifts are so long and he has to carry sixty pounds of stuff around. And it's crazy there. Everything's blown up, and he can't tell the bad guys from the good guys." I looked at Jack and stopped.

"Yeah?"

"Yeah. But he's okay. He'll probably come home with a Purple Heart, right, Jack?"

"Tell him we're playing Centerville in basketball, and we're going to kill them for him."

"Okay." I laughed. "I'll email him when we get home."

"He's not missing the weather, that's for sure." Don started up the hill toward a parking lot by two low brick buildings. "Is here good?"

"Perfect."

"I'll pick you guys up in an hour or so. Have fun."

As we got out, Don grinned at Jack. "Good talking to you, buddy."

We walked up the bigger hill, our footprints fresh in the new snow. I pulled the toboggan. There were a few younger kids sledding with their parents on the small hill. They looked like balls of pink, blue, and green in their snowsuits. When we got to the top, Kim stood with her arms spread out. "All right, before we go down, we have to think *Christmas*. We'll all close our eyes and try to see Christmas. All the things you think of when you think of Christmas."

I watched Kim and Jack close their eyes, and I closed mine too.

I thought about Christmas and remembered being at the top of this same hill with Sef on this same toboggan. I tried my hardest to remember every detail. Sonia was sledding, too. I remembered now that Van was behind me because as we started off she asked, "Aren't you scared, Cassie?"

"No," I said. We took off, and the sky was white, and the trees flashed by. Sef was in the back, yelling, "You will fly to success!" That was what his fortune cookie had said the night before.

Even while flying down the hill with the snow blowing in my face, I never thought anything bad could happen to us. Sonia had been too scared to sled. She walked down the hill and waited until we were done. She was probably cold too. I remembered thinking that I had Sef, and she didn't. I always had Sef. He would never let anything bad happen to us.

When I was little, I thought my life would always be soaring through the snow with Sef. Part of me wished I could stay in that place forever. Why would I want to know what lay ahead? Why would I want to know that Sef was going to leave? But I didn't want to be like Mom, pretending things were one way when they weren't. I wondered whether Christmas was the dream that somehow I'd still be flying downhill on that sled with Sef, or if it was seeing what was right here in front of us.

Suddenly the light shifted as a cloud passed over the sun. Kim asked, "Who saw Christmas?"

Jack's eyes shone. He lifted his arms and waved them high in the air. He danced and blew white streams into the air.

We laughed, and Kim said, "Let's go find it, then!"

Jack sat in the front of the toboggan, his legs tucked into the curve of wood. Kim was in the middle, and I pushed us off. Kim screamed the whole way. I called out, "You will fly to success!"

"Success" echoed behind us as we glided into the white.

HOLE

WHEN I GOT home, I opened my email. There was a message from Sef.

To: Mom, Dad, Van, Cassie
From: Sef
Subject: No Subject

Hi everyone,

I know I should wait to tell you this, but I can't. If I call in the next few days, then I want you to know. Please don't say anything to Jack.

A few nights ago I think I shot and killed a boy. But everyone was shooting at the same time, and it was dark, so there's a chance it wasn't me. I don't know exactly what happened. There was shooting, and we returned fire. I shot in that direction. Then I saw him fall.

As soon as it was quiet, I went over and saw a boy with a hole right between his eyes. He had a Yankees shirt on. Can you believe that? He shouldn't have been there at all. It was night, and the shooting started again, and we had to find cover fast. When we went back later, he was gone. But I can't get him out of my head. I mean I see him all the time. I wake at night and see him. He was only a little older than Jack.

I'd like to think he died instantly, that's what they say to the relatives of anyone who dies here, even if they're screaming in pain for hours. But I don't know. I haven't been able to eat or anything. What am I going to do? I don't think he even had a weapon. He was just standing there, in the wrong place at the wrong time. Everyone says to stop thinking like this because it's not anyone's fault. Hurricane says if I don't stop beating myself up, he's going to beat the crap out of me. I don't know, I just feel like I did it. I can't push it away.

I used to think things could be right if I tried hard enough. But that's not true here. I'm trying, and these guys are the best, but I don't know what we're doing here. I feel like a different person from the one who left. Write back and tell me things are better there.

Love,
Sef

He didn't do it, I thought, he couldn't have killed someone. But he felt like he did it, and the boy was dead, and no one could change that. I felt sick. I knew I could never tell Blue Sky. That was what she lived with every day. How could she understand it? That was why she blamed us. The boy didn't do anything except stand outside at the wrong time. But it wasn't Sef's fault—he would never kill a boy. It was just bad luck.

Sef was someone else now. It felt like there was a hole in my chest.

I put my sneakers on and ran. I ran all the way back to the state hospital. I stared at the snowy hills, waiting for something to come to me—a memory of Sef—something I could hold on to and take with me. I tried to see him, but all I could see was Mom happy and laughing when he was home.

As I was standing there at the bottom of the hill, Jesus pulled out of the state hospital parking lot. Would he be able to help Sef if Sef came home messed up? Would he be able to fix this tear inside me? I waved to the shaking, rumbling truck, but Jesus didn't see me.

On the way home, I saw Finn driving by in his Rabbit. There was someone in the front seat with him, and it wasn't Van. This girl was blond. I watched his lights disappear.

Van was asleep when I got home, but after I showered and was getting dressed in Sef's room, I felt someone watching me. Van was standing in the doorway. She had dark rings under her eyes. She was staring out the window. Just staring into the gray afternoon, the nothing. I shivered. My arms and legs were covered in goose bumps.

"Van?" I said. "What are you doing?"

Her eyes shifted toward me. She stepped back, as if she was startled. "I thought at first—it was so strange—I thought you were Sef for a minute. That he came home."

To: Sef
From: Cassie
Subject: Re: No Subject

Hi Sef,

Thanks for writing. I hardly know what to say. We all know whatever happened the night that boy was shot, you did the only thing you could do. Not that it makes it any better. I can't imagine how you must feel.

I'm scared too. It's hard to imagine you over there now. I know you have your team, but I wish we could do something. What can we do? Did you find out the boy's name? Do you want us to send money to his family? Let me know. I want to help. We all do. It's hard to be here and feel useless. I want to be there for you like you always were for us.

Thanks, Sef—I don't know if I've ever said it—for everything. I don't want to get all mushy, but I do want to say that you're the one who matters more to me than anything in the world. Why haven't I ever said that before? Because it's hard, I guess.

We're all doing OK. We just want you to be OK. I hope you are able to sleep. You did the only thing you could do.

And one last thing. Guess what I yelled when I was sledding with Kim and Jack today? "You will fly to success!"

Remember? It was great. Don dropped us off. He said to tell you they're going to crush Centerville for you. Please write back.

It's cold and icy. You're not missing anything. We're missing you.

Hang in there!

Love,

C

What if something happened to him before he got it? It could be the last time I ever got to write to him. Suddenly I was scared for him over there, really scared. Sef would go crazy if he kept seeing that dead boy. Or worse, if he gave up trying to make a difference.

CHAPTER 34

INSIDE A SNOW GLOBE

EVERYONE ELSE MUST have read Sef's email by now, I thought. He'd sent it last night. As soon as I got downstairs, the phone rang. Whenever the phone rang, we stopped what we were doing and waited to hear what Mom said next. She said hello, glanced back at us, and walked out of the room. Jack and I followed her. In between pauses, she said, "We're all doing fine, thanks. Sef's as good as can be expected. . . . That's right." She wore her party smile as she walked through the house with the phone.

"Oh, you did? We must have been out," she went on. "No, Jack is a little sick. . . . Yes, he'd love to see you. We all would. Next time. We'll call as soon as he's back to himself again."

Jack frowned. His hands tightened. He froze.

"Who was that?" I asked when she hung up.

"I'll tell you later," she mouthed.

"Was it Greg?"

"Later."

"Jason?"

She walked out of the room. I followed her into the living room.

"If Sef's friends are calling, we want to see them."

She turned fast and pointed her finger at me. "I don't want them to know Jack isn't talking, okay? I want to tell Sef that things are better here. And that's what I'm going to tell him because that's what he needs to hear."

"Maybe his friends could help."

"I'd rather keep it in the family."

"You read Sef's email then," I said.

She nodded quickly. "Not now."

"Ready to pick out a tree, Cass?" Dad called from the kitchen. He and Jack were in their coats by the door. I got in the car. "Mom's right, Cass. Not now," he said.

"When?"

"Let's get our tree first."

Jack picked out one that looked like it had been lying on its side all month. One side of it was flattened and brown. No matter how many others we showed him, he wanted that one. The tree man gave us a discount. On the way home, it started snowing tiny flakes like sparkles falling from the sky. Jack stuck his head out the window. He bit the air. Christmas was close, three days away, but it suddenly seemed as if it wasn't real anymore. As if it were just something I could shake inside a snow globe.

Mom barely looked up from the TV when we brought the tree in, or when Jack and I strung tinsel and lights and hung silver and gold balls.

Dad bent close to Mom so she could hear him over the TV. "Any plans for supper tonight?"

"Not really. I'm not hungry, are you?"

"We have to eat."

Jack went into the kitchen and sat at the table.

"Jack's hungry," I said. I stepped back from the tree. Every time I let my mind settle, I'd remember Sef and feel sick again.

Mom went in, opened the refrigerator, slapped a couple slices of cheese on a plate, and gave it to Jack. When she came back, I said softly, "Can I say something now?"

They looked up at me.

"What about Sef's email?"

"Poor Sef." Mom sighed. "Of course he didn't do it."

"Either way, he was just doing his job. You can't help anything like that. What else was he supposed to do? It's self-defense," Dad said.

"What are we going to do?" I asked.

They stared back at me. Dad clicked the volume down. He finally said, "What can we do? I wrote to Sef. What else can we do?"

"Something for Sef, something for the boy's family, I don't know. Something. I mean, someone's dead. What about his family?"

"Sef didn't do it," Mom said.

"Someone on his team did it," I said.

We could hear Jack opening and closing the refrigerator.

"When he calls, we can ask him what he wants us to do," Dad said.

"It could have been Sef who died," Mom said.

I shivered. "Don't say that, Mom."

"It wasn't Sef," Dad said.

"Well, I wouldn't want them to do anything for us," Mom said. "Besides, I know what I'm going to do. He needs to know that everything is okay here. That's what I'm going to tell him, and nobody better tell him otherwise."

"If everything's so okay, then why don't you at least make supper for Jack?" I said.

Mom glanced to the doorway, where Jack was staring at us.

Van pushed the kitchen door open. Snow sparkled on her dark hair. Her eyes were wide and bright. She seemed to carry all the secrets from the outside world, which was so much bigger than our inside world. "Hi," she said, spinning around to shut the door.

"Hi, Van," Dad said, letting his hand with the remote fall to his side.

"Have you been drinking again?" Mom asked.

"What?" Van said.

"Van," she said, "I noticed a few things missing from the liquor cabinet. Do you know anything about it?"

"No."

"Then who does?"

"I don't know." Van slid off her black suede coat. She looked from Dad to me and back to Mom.

Dad motioned to me with his hand, waving me away. Jack and I went up to Sef's room. I left the door open.

"No cell phone for two weeks," I heard Mom say. "You're grounded and no cell. Things are going to get better around here."

Van yelled, "You're not exactly making things better!"

Van never yelled. Jack came up behind me and took my hand. Van came running up the stairs. Then she stopped and threw her phone. It smashed off the wall and bounced down the stairs.

I looked down at Jack. His arms slid around my waist, and he pushed his face close.

After Jack fell asleep, I went into our room. Van was lying on her bed, staring at the ceiling.

"Did you read Sef's email?" I sat on my bed.

"Yeah."

"You okay?"

"Yeah."

"You sure?"

"Yes, I'm sure." She turned toward me. Her eyes were red.

"What are you going to do?"

"I don't know. I was so worried about Sef getting shot, I didn't even think about the other way around."

She stared without blinking, then her face crumpled up and she covered her face and started to cry. Her body shook up and down. I put my hand on her back because I wasn't sure what else to do. I could feel her ribs beneath my fingers. She was all bones. I said, "It's okay."

"I can't believe he killed someone," she whispered. "A boy."

"It might not have been Sef," I said.

"He's still dead," Van said.

"I know."

We sat there in the quiet dark for a long time, wondering who might die next.

DIGNITY

MOM TRIED HARD to hold herself together and make things nice for Christmas. She hung wreaths, played Christmas music, and made a ham dinner and chocolate pie, which made Dad and Jack happy. All Christmas morning, she smiled like she was at a party. We watched Jack open his presents. Once when he was unwrapping some toy soldiers with real camouflage outfits, his mouth opened wide and I thought he was going to scream something out, but he didn't. On Christmas afternoon, Dad carried his few things out of Jack's room and stripped the bed. Then he came downstairs, whistling "My Bonnie Lies over the Ocean," and poured drinks for him and Mom. Mom put down Sef's high school graduation picture and held Dad's hand.

Later in Sef's room, I thought of all the Christmases when he was here. Shadows flitted across the walls of his room. Birds, I thought. Outside my window, the feeder Sef made was careening back and forth in the wind. I went down to the kitchen and found some ends of bread that I tore into pieces. I leaned out the window and stuffed the bread crumbs into the little wooden box.

The day after Christmas, Dad said he'd take us to see the Russian circus. Someone at work had given him four tickets. Mom stayed at home to rest. As we backed out of the driveway, he said, "Who's going to have a good time today?"

Jack waved his arms in the air. He banged the back of Dad's car seat.

"That's what I want to hear. Cass? Van? What about you?"

"We're going to have a good time," I said, "even though I don't know what a Russian circus is."

"You'll find out. Van?"

Van sighed. "Are we supposed to assume that everything is just fine and dandy, and off to the circus we go to have a great time?"

"We're trying."

She sighed. "That's it? That's all you're going to say?"

"Listen, Van, don't think I don't think about Sef and all this"—he waved his hand around—"every second of the day, because I do. But we need each other. There's too much going on. I think you know what I mean."

"I know what you mean, but it's not fair," Van said. "Mom puts up some decorations and cooks a stupid ham for Christmas, and everything's supposed to be fine again."

"It's like *Animal Farm*," I said. "All animals are equal except pigs are more equal."

Dad chuckled.

"It's not funny," Van said. "What about us?"

"Okay," he said. "What do you want me to do?"

"I think if she really wants to make everything okay, then she should stop drinking so much and taking so many pills. Why don't you ground *her*?" Van said. "Okay, kidding about that, but not about the rest."

Dad nodded.

"Van's right," I said. "Why do we keep pretending everything's fine?"

"It takes time. We're working on it." Dad glanced in the rearview mirror at Jack. "We can talk more tonight."

"Promise?" Van asked.

"Yes."

"You're not going to just give in to her like you always do?"

"Do I do that?" Dad grinned and drove fast down the Mass Pike toward the Worcester Centrum.

It felt like we were waiting for a basketball game or a concert until the lights went down, the music came on, and the announcer presented the "Great Moscow Circus!" Tiny white lights sparkled from the ceiling like it was snowing. Jack kept standing to see the clown with the red nose and leather cap, and Dad kept sitting him back down. Jack smiled and clapped hard for the beautiful acrobats, the white tigers, the horses dashing in circles, the eight men riding a bike, and his face exploded when he saw the big brown bear dancing.

At first I thought the bear with his frilly pink skirt that matched the tightrope walker's was fake, but he lumbered as he danced, and when he stopped, he opened his mouth wide and made a low, hollow sound that no human could make. He danced faster as the orchestra played, shaking his shaggy brown head as he followed the pretty tightrope walker around the ring, taking treats from her hand. The thump of his feet sounded through the arena. Then he picked her up and carried her in his big brown arms to the spotlight in the center of the ring. He set her down and bowed.

"Dad," Van said, "bears shouldn't be doing that."

Dad stopped eating his popcorn. "It's just a show, Van. Don't worry. Try to enjoy it."

"It's not right. He's a bear."

"Well, he's Russian," he joked.

Van wouldn't watch the bears. She covered her face. After the show, Dad decided to buy a Russian fur hat and we took pictures in front of the circus banner.

Mom had supper of roasted chicken, potatoes, and salad ready when we got home. "Smells great in here, honey," Dad said, raising his eyebrows at me and Van. He went up behind Mom and held her shoulders and kissed her neck. "I'm starving."

"Good," she said.

"For you, I mean. Can I eat you up?" Dad said.

"Dad, please," Van said. "That's disgusting."

"Yeah, Dad," I said. "Gross."

"All right, all right," he said, patting his belly.

"A real Casanova until he sees the food." Mom smiled with her hands on her hips.

We all sat down.

"How was the circus?"

Jack pounded his silverware on the table, stabbing his fork into the wood.

"So you liked it, Jack?" Mom nodded. "Anyone else have anything to say?"

Dad looked up. "Does it have to be nice?"

Mom sighed. "You know the rule." The rule was, If you don't have something nice to say, then don't say anything.

"Well, the girls have a few things they want to say."

"Oh?" Mom said. "About the circus?"

"Not exactly," Van said. "But just so you know, the circus was great, except for the dancing bear that didn't even look like a bear. He had this stupid frilly outfit on."

"No one liked the dancing bear?" Mom asked, surprised.

"I did," Dad said. "He carried the pretty woman."

"Because she fed him snacks," I said.

"So?" Dad said. "It was romantic."

I burst out laughing. "Lucky Mom, if that's your idea of romance."

Mom laughed, too.

Van ripped a roll in half. "A bear should be a bear."

"Jack's with me. He loved it—right, buddy?" Dad said.

Jack scowled at us and thumped his knife.

"What about you, Cassie? What'd you think?"

I put down my forkful of potato. "I liked the horses the best, but Van's right. The bear was kind of sad. He had this big red bow on. He looked silly. Like a clown. Bears should have some dignity."

"I hate to tell you, Cass," Dad said, "but people do much worse things."

"That still doesn't make it right," I said.

"That's true," Dad said. "We should all have a little dignity."

Jack slid off his seat and walked into the living room and pressed Play on the DVD player.

"Guess he's done." Mom reached for her prescription bottle on the counter behind her.

Van asked, "Mom, why do *you* take so many pills?"

"Oh, is this what we're talking about again?" Mom picked up her glass of wine. "They relax me when I feel stressed out. That's why the doctor prescribes them for me."

"Are you supposed to take them while you drink?"

"What is this?" Mom demanded. "I feel like I'm being interrogated, and I'm the adult here."

"Well, I've been thinking," Van said slowly. "Whether you realize it or not, you are setting an example for us."

No one said anything. Looney Tunes music blasted from the living room. Dad stabbed his chicken and pushed it into his mouth.

"That's true, but I took these after Jack was born because I needed them. And now I'm taking them again. I don't want to be a nervous wreck all the time," Mom said. She set her glass down and pushed her hair back. "I'm trying to do my best, that's all I can do. I'm going to try to make things"—she paused and looked at me—"okay again. Really okay."

"We just want things to be fair." I looked at Van. "I mean, normal again. I don't know if they'll ever be normal for Sef again, but things should be more normal for us."

"Yeah," Van said. "Can things be better for us and not just *because of* Sef? It seems like everything's for Sef, which I get. But we have to think of us too."

"Okay. Your father and I are trying to work this out." Mom's face pinched up. "I should be more responsible. I should think of how you feel—I'm sorry. It just hurt so much. It still does."

Dad squeezed her hand and nodded. Outside, the wind blew the frozen snow against the windows. *Spat, spat.*

"Everyone else hurts, too, Mom," Van said. "We all do."

Mom stared at Van. Van never said this much.

"We'll take care of us. We'll make things better for all of us," Dad said. "And Sef will be home before we know it. We want him to come home to the place he left. He needs that."

Upstairs, Jack was drooling in his sleeping bag. He wasn't moving, but his eyes were open. "Hi, Jack," I said. "It's Supergirl here to tell you that everything's going to be okay. Can you hear me? You sure don't look very dignified right now, but everything's going to be all right." I waited for him to look at me, but he didn't. "I wonder what you thought of the dancing bear today. I thought I saw you laughing, but maybe it made you really mad. Maybe you can talk to me tomorrow. That sound good? Supergirl says yes, that sounds good. I don't know how long I can be Supergirl, but I'm trying. It's hard to be that good.

"Good night, Jack." I paused. "Roger that."

CHAPTER 36

HAPPY NEW YEAR!

Bly Sky's Blog

December 30, 2006

Today is the first day of Eid and the news is shock. This was happy day in past. It was big surprise to know Saddam was executed this morning. No one like him for horrible things he did but he was President for 35 years. Why they can not wait until the end of Eid? Even your Bush not execute on Christmas day, true? The worse is the guards told him to go to hell and taunt him at the end. It is not right. Everyone is sad about it. I take my breakfast of hot bread, tea, milk, cream, yogurt and eggs. We learn about Saddam and now no appetite.

Normally at Eid we clean the house. Of course we need water to clean. When the water started as a trickle this morning we dance and collect all we can before it stop. It is never enough.

We pray everyday and hope it work real good.

To: Blue Sky
From: Cassie
Subject: Happy New Year

Dear Blue Sky,

I am writing to say Happy New Year and Happy Eid, but
first I have to say sorry Saddam Hussein had to die the way
he did. No one should die like that. It's not right. How can so
many things go wrong in your country?

How is your family? Any news? I hope you are still there
and can email back. I wish you a happy and safe 2007. I have
an assignment for social studies to interview someone from
another country. Could I interview you? I hope so. Write back
soon if you can.

Your friend,

Cassie

To: Cassie
From: Blue Sky
Subject: Re: Happy New Year

Dear Cassie,

Yes, it is possible to interview. Send the questions soon.
The problem is we leave here. If we stay we can not be safe.
America can not protect us. Supervisor of my father say the
good Iraqis need to stay to rebuild Iraq but he can not help
us. We talk about Syria or Jordan. They are the only countries
to take us without visa. Have to be careful the next days or we
might die. I fill my suitcase. We are ready.

What memories I save? What CDs, videos, pictures, stuffed animals. Yes I take my computer. Can I use it? Will we ever be come back again? I get scared. What happens to Iraq? Most of our family is here. I do not want to leave them. My mother cry and cry about my uncle. No word and she has terrible time leave him to die. Who bury him? she ask over and over. But my father says we need go fast. Something worse happen in that time we wait.

And school? It is better to live but I need education more than anything. I have dreams. I choose life.

We check for driver reliable to take us. We could take a plane but the Baghdad Airport is very dangerous. Terrorists are like a disease. No one stop them. They pretend to do this for religion but they have no belief. It is dangerous to live.

May peace come soon to Iraq.

Regards,

Blue Sky

To: Blue Sky
From: Cassie
Subject: Re: Re: Happy New Year

Dear Blue Sky,

How do you leave everything you know? I hope it all works out for your family. I am going to pray for you. I am scared for you. And I'm afraid I won't hear from you anymore.

Here is the list of interview questions. I know the answers to a lot of them now, so just answer what you can. I am going to present you to my class. I want everyone to know who you are, and what is happening in your country. I know you might have to leave quickly. That's OK.

1. What is your blog name, what does it mean, and why did you start your blog?

2. What is your first memory?

3. What is your everyday life like there, and how has the war changed the way you live your life?

4. What are your favorite foods?

5. What is your favorite subject in school? Least favorite?

6. Do you have brothers and sisters?

7. What do your parents do?

8. What do you want to do when you are older?

9. What would you like to tell the world about you/Iraq?

10. What are your dreams?

I keep thinking about what you said about hope. I have been trying to believe in something so the rest will follow. I am trying to be Supergirl like you. Please be safe and write if you can.

> Your friend,
> Cassie

CHAPTER 37

DYING

WHEN I SAW the picture of Saddam Hussein with the noose around his neck, I felt sorry for him, even though I knew he did so many horrible things. Mom wouldn't look at the newspaper when I showed her. She said, "It's about time. He's nothing but a rat who deserves to die." Dad said, "That's what happens in a war. Besides, it was the Iraqis who decided to do it."

I stopped eating my cereal. "We wanted him executed. They probably got paid to do it. On the first day of Eid, too."

"What is *Eid*?" Mom asked.

"It's like their Christmas." I held up the paper to Dad. "Look at him."

"I saw him." Dad threw up his arms. "How can you feel sorry for Saddam Hussein? He threw his people into vats of chemicals and hung them from ceilings by hooks! He tortured thousands of his own people!"

"It's still not right," I said.

"I don't care as long as it means Sef can home quicker," Mom said. "Maybe now the war will end."

"Don't count on it," Dad said.

"That country is crazy. I don't know what he's doing there at all." Mom began to cry. "He's going to be all messed up."

Dad shot me a look, took the paper, folded it, and put it into his armpit. "He's going to be fine. He's going to be the same Sef he always was."

The back of my cereal box read, "How long can a puffin stay underwater?" I stared at the cartoon bird with the big beak. I kept seeing the picture of Saddam with the noose around his neck in the paper. How could anyone *want* someone to die?

"Remember Blue Sky, the girl from Iraq who wrote the blog? Her family has to leave Iraq."

"Why?" Dad asked.

"Her father worked for our military as a translator. If they don't leave, they could be killed. They might be killed anyway."

"I thought things were starting to get better over there." Mom sighed. "Do you even know if Blue Sky is real?"

"Are you kidding? You actually think someone's pretending to be an Iraqi girl?" I laughed.

"Well, we're over there fighting for them. Sef is risking his life. Does your friend realize that?"

"She realizes it every time a bomb falls, which is all day long— or *was* all day long. I'm not sure where she is now."

Mom threw up her hands. "Her father's working for us, probably making more money than he's ever made, and you're telling me they don't want us there?"

" *Was* working for us before his family was threatened and had to leave their country. And we can't help them. Or won't help them."

"Come on, Cassie. We're spending billions of dollars over there. They aren't grateful for that?" Mom said. "It's not like we're threatening them."

"Just listen to her, Grace," Dad said. "Let her talk."

"She said her father had a good job before the war. He was an English teacher. They could leave their house then. They weren't in danger of getting shot or blown up every time they did leave. Now after he's worked for us for three years, we can't help them."

Mom took a deep breath. "Cassie," she said slowly, "did it ever cross your mind that we've got enough on our plate already? At least *I* do."

I thought about what Blue Sky had said—that they didn't show Iraqis dying on our TVs. We knew troops were dying, but we didn't see them either. They were only numbers in the paper. I ran down the street where the cars had cleared tracks. I ran up and down our street until I was too tired to be scared about Blue Sky or Sef anymore. I was like the polar bear I saw once at a zoo in New York, swimming in circles, pushing off the wall over and over again.

Then I fell back into the snow on our lawn under the gray sky and lay there until I could breathe right. I looked up once and saw Van in the window. I half waved to her, and she disappeared.

Van was lying on her bed with her book over her face. "Hey," I said. "You okay?"

"No. I feel like I'm dying," she said through the book. "Finn's going to break up with me."

"How do you know?"

"I know. He thinks I'm crazy."

"What do you mean?"

She stared at me. "This is the worst New Year's ever. I really don't feel like staying here all night. It's going to be so boring."

"Yeah, I know what you mean."

"This is the first time I'm going to miss Nora's party."

"Why don't you call her on my cell phone?"

"Maybe I will."

I could hear Nora's voice as Van walked out of our room. "I mean he's cool, but does he respect you, and I mean *R-E-S-P-E-C-T?*"

Down the hall, Van shut the bathroom door behind her. I went into Sef's room, where Jack was sitting on the floor with Mom's poetry books stacked all around him. On the top was one called *The Colossus,* and on top of that was the picture of Sef driving a tank that Mom had printed. Sef was smiling and waving, but the tank looked like some kind of enormous metal contraption that was swallowing him.

A circle shape outlined where the Osama bin Laden dartboard had been. Jack must have taken it down. There were hundreds of tiny holes and longer scrapes where the darts hit or dragged over Sef's door. I ran my finger over them.

After a while, Van finally came out of the bathroom, walked back to our room, and shut the door. The long, beautiful dark hair that she'd had her whole life was chopped off. My stomach turned. What'd she do? In the bathroom, I brushed my foot through the piles of dark, feathery hair without a sound. It looked like someone had died.

When I went into our room, Van was looking in the mirror.

"You okay?"

She laughed a high, strained laugh. "I can't believe I just did that. What do you think?"

"It actually looks good." I was surprised. Van looked even more beautiful than before. Her short, choppy hair framed her small face, made each feature look more perfect.

"Yeah? Feels pretty good, but I'll probably kill myself in the morning." She ran her fingers through her hair like a comb. "I better clean up before Mom thinks an animal was skinned in there."

"Well, at least it's not a boring New Year's Eve," I said.

She laughed again, and I realized that I hadn't heard her laugh in so long.

Mom gasped when she saw Van. "What happened?"

"I cut my hair." Van was smiling.

"What is going to happen next around here?" Mom sat down and then looked up to Van. "Why?"

"I just wanted to. Can you stop staring at me like that now?"

It was strange. There was something calm about Van—almost peaceful. Mom had long dark hair like Van that she twirled into a knot on the back of her head. She never would have cut her hair like that. Ever.

When Dad came in from the garage, he stopped and said, "Did you get your hair cut, Van?"

"Yes," she said. "I did it."

"Oh, it's nice."

Mom stood behind him with her mouth open.

"Thanks," Van said as she carried the dustpan up the stairs.

"Happy New Year!" Dad raised his glass.

Mom smiled a big broken smile and clinked her glass with his. "To 2007."

CHAPTER 38

REAL

KIM WAS ABSENT the first day back at school. Her plane back from visiting her father in LA had been delayed. Rob was out too, sick with the flu.

I stood in the middle of the cafeteria holding my carton of chocolate milk, trying to decide which direction to go. Dave Swanson was standing behind me. For days after the football game, he wouldn't look at me. Now all of a sudden, he was there whenever I turned around. I tried to ignore him.

Sonia was heading out of the lunch line with a salad on a tray. She was wearing the CHOOSE LIFE T-shirt that I gave her. Life was our favorite cereal. I stayed where I was on her path. She could have gone around me, but she didn't.

"Lost?" she asked.

"Very funny," I said. "Can I sit with you?"

"Whatever." She shrugged, but I saw a little glimmer in her eyes.

"Look who's back. Guess Weirdo's not here," Michaela said

when we reached their table. "It's been, like, months. I'm only getting like a C in math now, but whatever."

I said, "Weren't you getting a C before too?"

"Ha ha. Why does Dave Swanson keep looking over here?"

"How should I know?" I said.

"So, are you going to the Spring Dance with him?"

"Are you joking?"

"Well, I just thought you might want to know that I'm asking Rob."

Everyone looked at me.

"And do you think he'll say yes?" I asked her.

"What's that supposed to mean?" Michaela glared at me.

"Just that he never says yes to dances. Remember how many girls asked him last year?"

"And you're suddenly the expert on Rob," she said.

"Okay," Lisa said. "I think this is when it's, like, time for a new subject."

There was silence, then Lisa asked, "So is it true Jack almost got run over in the parking lot?"

"Yeah, that really icy week."

"That's so crazy. Is he all right?" She smiled a little, so I couldn't tell if she was making fun of us.

"He was a little shell-shocked, but he's fine now."

"First I heard Mr. Mac actually did run him over. I was so relieved he was okay," Sonia said. "Jack's a sweet kid."

"Thanks," I said.

Sonia looked away.

"He's lucky." Lisa set her Diet Coke down. "Did he stop talking or something?"

"He's just been having a hard time."

Michaela flipped her straightened hair over her shoulder. "Isn't your whole family kind of wacky?"

"I can't believe you said that," Sonia blurted out. "I never said that."

"Maybe not exactly in those words." Michaela smirked.

Sonia didn't say anything. She glanced from me to Michaela and back. I tried to eat my peanut butter and jelly sandwich, but the peanut butter stuck to the top of my mouth. Michaela slipped her math homework in front of me. Then she glossed her lips sparkling pink.

"I have to go," I said.

"Where do you have to go?" Sonia asked.

"Somewhere real."

Sonia lifted her silver-blue eyes. "Right."

"Let me know if you want to talk sometime," I said to Sonia, and left.

CHAPTER 39

YOU CAN TALK

ON THE BUS home from school, I heard Ben Adams talking to a friend. "That's the retard. He hasn't said anything—nothing—since I told him he better shut up or else I'd make sure his brother never came back from Iraq." They laughed.

I turned to Jack. "Did Ben tell you not to tell anyone what he did to you or he'd make sure Sef never came home?"

Jack looked up with wide eyes, squeezed his lips together, and sucked them inside his mouth.

"He won't hurt you again. He won't." I wanted to kill Ben right there. "Do you really think he could do anything to hurt Sef?"

Jack looked down.

"There's no way. Do you want me to tell Sef what he said?"

He shook his head.

"Then you have to start talking again. I mean it. Sef would tear him to pieces in about five seconds."

The bus jerked to a stop. When Ben stood up behind us to get off, I stepped into the aisle, blocking it. "I know what you did to Jack."

"So?"

"So, you're not going to get away with it. And if you touch him again—"

"I'm really scared."

I knew I was causing a traffic jam. "Let me by," Ben said.

Mr. Fletcher turned around in his seat. "What's the problem back there?"

"You better wait for me when we get off the bus, or I'm going to your house. Do you understand?"

Ben stood there.

"Say it, then."

"I understand."

We started down the aisle.

Jack walked off the bus after Ben without a word. I wanted to scoop him up and bicycle him far away from here. But I knew even then that I couldn't really protect him. Just like Sef couldn't protect me anymore.

Kristen had already started walking home. She stopped when she saw me put my arm in front of Ben. I said, "You need to say sorry."

Ben stood there.

"I could tell your mother right now, like you told on me, and make you come over and apologize for punching Jack and threatening him, but I'm not a little tattletale. Now, look at him," I said.

Ben stared at Jack's feet.

"In the eyes," I said. My voice was harder than I knew. It

didn't even feel like my own. "And tell him you're not going to touch him again and Sef will be fine."

Ben did. Jack smiled fiercely.

"What's going on?" Kristen asked Ben.

"Nothing."

"Did you do something to Jack?"

"Not really."

"Only beat him up and told him if he said anything that Sef wouldn't come home," I said.

"Come on, you big jerk." Kristen yanked Ben's arm and pulled him toward their driveway. Ben's face pinched up like he was going to cry.

I almost liked Kristen right then.

On the way home, I turned to Jack, smiling wide. I waited for him to say something.

"Listen, Jack, you can talk now. Go ahead."

He shook his head.

"You don't really think that Ben could have any power over Sef, do you? No way. Never. Really, you can talk. Even Ben said so. Try it."

He turned and frowned at me.

"Okay. As soon as you're ready, Jack," I said.

The next day Kim was back at school. I was so glad, I ran up and hugged her. I could hardly wait until lunch. I met her at her locker, and we walked to the cafeteria. I said, "I don't know where to begin."

"I saw Van walking home yesterday," she said. "I guess she got her hair cut."

"She did it herself on New Year's Eve." I told her the whole story.

"Well, at least she did something," she said.

"What do you mean?"

"I mean she cut her hair. She's doing something instead of nothing. She's making a statement."

We got our chocolate milks and sat down. Kim ate a forkful of noodles and broccoli.

"She did seem happier afterward, but I don't think she is," I said. "I might need to give her Jesus's card."

Kim looked at me like I was crazy.

"Just kidding," I said. "Did I tell you I saw him pulling out of the state hospital the other day?"

"That figures." She sucked up the rest of her chocolate milk. "The Lord is my shepherd. There is nothing I shall want. Except a Dunkin' Donuts coffee and chocolate doughnut, and my meds and a shrink."

We laughed.

"He will rise again—and never work another day in his life," she kept going between laughing. "Wait until I tell my mom he was at the state hospital."

"How'd it go with your dad?" I asked.

She sighed. "It made me wish my parents had tried to work it out. But they used to fight all the time, so it's probably for the best. It's hard to have a relationship with someone who's never here and then doesn't know what to do when I'm all of a sudden there."

"Yeah," I said, "it's hard enough when they are there all the time."

She smiled and ate her noodles.

"Can I tell you about Ben Adams?"

"It was him, wasn't it?"

"Don't worry," she said after I told her the whole story. "Jack will talk when he's ready."

"I hope so."

Dave Swanson was standing behind us. "Oh, hey, Dave," Kim said. "Do you need anything?"

"No." He frowned and walked away.

"That was weird. Guess that's what comes with being a math genius," I said.

"Or maybe he's thinking of asking you to the Spring Dance."

"Don't even say it."

Kristen Adams stopped at our table. "Listen, I just want to say I'm sorry about whatever Ben did to Jack. I hope he's okay."

"He's okay."

"You're not going to say anything, are you? My dad's pretty hard on him."

I remembered Mr. Adams's angry voice that night I apologized to Ben. *She's only a girl, for crissake.*

"No, I'm not going to. Is he okay?"

"Yeah, he's okay. Thanks, Cassie," she said.

The bell rang, and Kim and I left for English.

"I can't believe Kristen Adams just apologized to me." I laughed.

"Hey, stranger things can happen. And you're Supergirl, after all," Kim said. "By the way, have you talked to Rob?"

"A couple of emails, that's it. He's sick."

"Lovesick?"

"Very funny. Actually, I think he forgot all about me over break."

"Have you done anything?"

"No."

"Well, maybe he thinks the same thing about you."

I turned to her. "You know what? It was too quiet around here when you were gone."

"Well, Big Mouth Kim's back." She laughed. "I missed you too. I kept wanting to tell you things."

"Really?"

"Yeah."

"Did you write them down?"

She shook her head.

"Next time," I said.

Van spent the weekend crying in her room. The breakup was official. "You can talk to me if you want, Van," I said quietly. She didn't answer. "Maybe later," I said.

At supper she barely ate anything. Her face was like stone. She said to Mom, "If you hadn't grounded me, it wouldn't have happened."

"Oh, no, honey," Mom said. "That's not fair."

Mom placed Van's phone on the table, two weeks from the day Van had thrown it against the wall. It hadn't broken. Van just stared at it. "I'm sorry, honey," Mom said.

When Dad got home, he put his arm around her shoulders and said, "You have to live your life, Van. Besides, you're too good for him."

"No, I'm not!"

I said, "Remember what Sef said right before he left? He said not to let anyone get you down. You promised him."

Van half shrugged.

"Listen, I know you like him, but you can't let him do this to you." Dad's eyes rolled back, and he mumbled, "And he can't sing."

"What?" Van said. "What'd you say?"

"Van, he doesn't even know any Sinatra." Dad belted out, "The summer wind came blowin' in—from across the sea—"

Mom burst out laughing. She held her hand over her mouth and said, "Sorry. I'm not laughing at you, Van. I'm laughing at your father."

Van stood so fast, she knocked over her chair. "I hate it here! I hate it!"

CHAPTER 40

EXECUTION MEAL

Bly Sky's Blog

January 3, 2007

This is truth. No one is happy about a thing until it is lost. Until it disappear and you live without it. This is true of electricity, water, Iraq, peace, and blue sky. Today I am to sad to write. I want to be a girl who live in Iraq only. That ask to much?

To: Mom, Dad, Van, Cassie
From: Sef
Subject: No Subject

Hi everyone,

Thanks for all your emails. Thanks for the awesome package, Cass. That was great. You made a lot of us happy. Oh, yeah, and Merry Christmas and Happy New Year! Sorry I didn't call. It was crazy trying to get through on the phone.

I'll call soon. I want to talk to Jack this time. I missed you last time, buddy. How was it?

The last 2 weeks were long and hard. I'm so tired all the time. I wish I brought that Pink Floyd CD I used to listen to. Maybe you could send it. I used to go to sleep listening to that. I've been listening to too much AC/DC and Metallica. Never thought I'd be a metalhead! Tim plays them all the time.

Did I tell you after that we planned our execution meals? Don't panic, Mom, it's just for fun. I'm going to keep these guys safe if it's the last thing I do, and they'll do the same for me. Hurricane wants roast beef, rolls, asparagus, baked potatoes with onions, and for dessert, ice cream sundaes and Bud. Mark said he'd have fried chicken with the works— mashed potatoes, corn bread, beans, and everything else. For dessert he wanted Snowballs, those squishy pink things covered with coconut! Who would ever choose that for the last thing they ate? Tim wanted beef stew, Coors, and Oreo cookies covered in whipped cream. I wanted Mom's spaghetti and meatballs and Fresh's chocolate pie.

Everyone doing OK? Sounds like it. I'm OK too. Nights are hard still. I'm trying not to think too much.

Love,

Sef

After we both read it, I turned to Van. "Does it seem like he's not telling us something?"

"Yeah, like did he kill that boy or not?" She stared into my eyes. "That's why he hasn't called, and that's why he's not talking about it."

"He does say the nights are hard still," I said. "Maybe he doesn't know anything else."

"Probably he wishes he never told us about it to begin with."

"Remember that three-legged dog?"

"Of course."

"He never talked about that again either."

"I'm scared," Van said.

"Me too," I said.

"Is this the kind of thing he thinks about every day for the rest of his life?"

"I know. How could he stop thinking about it?"

"Sef emailed!" Mom sang out from down the hallway. We heard her footsteps and then she stepped into the doorway of our room. "Didn't you hear me? Sef emailed." She looked from me to Van. "So why's it like a morgue in here?"

The next few days, it snowed off and on, each time covering the ice that had already turned sooty black. White to grayish black and then back again. I didn't hear from Blue Sky, and we didn't hear from Sef. It seemed like all we did was wait to hear from Iraq.

CHAPTER 41

TRUTH OR TRUTH

"VAN! VAN!" I called. "I have to go! The movie starts at one."

I hadn't seen her since Mom and Dad left over an hour ago, and she was supposed to babysit Jack. After I searched the inside of the house and the garage, I asked Jack if he'd seen her. He pointed at the window.

"Outside?"

He nodded, not looking away from *Tom and Jerry*.

"Where outside?"

He pointed again, toward the backyard.

"Out back? Are you sure?"

He didn't answer.

The bright sun was melting the snow-crusted ice, breaking up every time I took a step. I had on my sneakers, and I could feel the snow inside my socks. I stood in the backyard, staring into the sun glaring off the window of our room, as if Van was just suddenly going to appear there. I called Kim on my cell to tell her I couldn't leave Jack until I found Van.

I started to turn when I felt someone behind me, like a shadow. I knew it was Van. She was lying in a hole of snow the shape of her body. It looked as if she might have been trying to make a snow angel, but she wasn't spreading her arms and legs. She was still, and her skin was white, and her hands were folded into a ball on top of her chest.

"Van!" I ran through the snow and yanked her up by her frozen arm. Her T-shirt and pajama bottoms were iced over.

"Open your eyes! Please!"

She blinked, and her eyes opened, dark and bright.

"Say something!" I waited, holding her. I could feel her bones through her T-shirt. "How long have you been out here?"

Her blue lips parted slightly, but nothing came out.

"Come on, what are you doing? What's the matter with you? Are you crazy?" I shook her. "You need to get inside. Now! Help me! You're so cold."

I tried to drag her in, but she was heavier than she looked. Tears rolled down my cheeks and fell into the snow. "What are you trying to prove? It's not fair—you have everything, and you're wasting it. And what for? Finn? Look at yourself, Van."

I should have known something like this could happen. I should have seen it coming.

Everything sparkled white around us. I lifted her up, and we stumbled along. I looked into her eyes. When she wasn't wearing her black boots, we were the same height. She had on her big brown monster slippers with the white claws, and that made me cry even more. Van looked horrified.

"Stop crying," she said. "You never cry."

"You scared me. I thought—I don't know, I thought— Come

213

on." I wiped my face and half pulled, half carried her through the back sliding glass door and upstairs into her bed. "Van, what were you trying to do?"

She lay on her bed, looking at the ceiling. She wrapped her arms around herself. I remembered reading in Sef's survival handbook to put as many blankets on a frozen person as possible, so I started piling them on—my comforter and blankets, Jack's, Sef's, Mom and Dad's—until Van was buried.

"Remember all the things you said you were going to do? You were going to travel and teach kids in other countries and work for Greenpeace. Remember?"

She raised her hands and spread them in the air like starfish. "Sorry. Please don't cry anymore," she said. "You're scaring me, and everything's tingling. I feel like I'm burning up."

"Where?"

"My fingers and ears sting."

"What about your nose? How long were you out there?"

"Not that long, maybe an hour. Is my nose swollen? It feels funny."

She was still shaking. Jack came in. He walked over and touched Van's face. He opened his mouth and breathed in a quick breath as if he was going to say something. She smiled a little.

"We have to warm her up. Stay here while I make some tea."

I made English Breakfast tea with milk and sugar. She took small sips while I sat next to her bed, watching her. Jack sat with us, making piles of screws, nails, coils of wire, wheels, and random scraps from his old metal collection.

"You can't tell anyone. Promise," she said.

"I promise if you promise never to do anything like that again."

She looked so pretty with her choppy dark hair falling around her pale face.

"It isn't what you think. I mean, I didn't want to die or anything. I was waiting for the numb part. That's what happens. I just didn't want to hurt anymore." She closed her eyes.

Jack kicked the metal pieces. He picked up handfuls and threw them across the room. They made clinking sounds as they hit the bed, the desk, and the window. Then he stood there with his hands in fists at his sides, his body stiff.

"Van's okay, Jack." I took his hand. "Luckily, you told me she was out back. She was waiting for us."

His body slowly released, and his arms went limp. His hands opened.

"Come on. You can watch some cartoons in Mom and Dad's room."

I wrapped White Kitty and Jack in the sheets and turned the TV on loud. When I got back to Van, I said, "I forgot about Jack."

She stretched her fingers, fluttered them over her head.

"I'm glad you're okay. I thought you were okay before, but I guess you weren't."

After a while, she looked up. "Do you ever have dreams that Sef is dead and you'll never see him again?"

"Yes," I said.

"I'm so scared sometimes. Everyone thinks all this is just about Finn, but it's not. I dream about Sef all the time. I wish he never went over there."

"I know. Me too."

Van rolled her head to the side. "I'm mad at Mom too. I know she's trying harder now, but everything is always about her. And Sef. She barely notices me. Because I'm the quiet one. You were never afraid of anything, but I was. I *am*. Everything always seems so easy for you. I wanted to be close to Sef like you—" She paused. "And I always wanted to look like you, too. Everyone always says I look just like Mom."

"Are you for real?" How could Van ever want to look like me?

She nodded and closed her eyes.

"Sure you're not hallucinating, Van? You're a thousand times prettier. Maybe a million."

She laughed. "You don't even know."

"And you *are* close to Sef. He's always looking out for you. He would kill Finn if he knew he'd hurt you."

Van smiled. "That's true."

"And one more thing. Nothing is easy. I *am* scared now. About everything."

Van closed her eyes. "I want to sleep now. I'm so tired."

"Okay. Can you do me a favor?"

She nodded.

"Keep talking to me when you wake up."

She smiled with her eyes closed. "Okay."

After she fell asleep, I traced a blue vein running under the soft warm skin of her forehead. I called Kim and told her everything.

"How could Van want to look like me?" I asked her.

"Hey, Supergirl, why don't you look in the mirror sometime," she said.

I did. I fingered the raised skin of the scar that curved down from my eyebrow. My eyes were pale blue like the color of the oceans of faraway beaches, as Mom once said. We were at the kitchen table, cutting pictures out of magazines. Mom held up the ad showing the clear blue water and white sand. "See, your eyes are this pale blue and you have long dark lashes. No one has those." Then she sighed and slapped the magazine down. "I don't know why I bother looking at these stupid ads. We'll never be able to go to those beaches."

I used to want to look like Mom and Van. Now I thought, *These are my eyes the color of the ocean, and this is my scar.* My eyes looked bigger and clearer. I looked like myself. I shook my hair out of my ponytail. Long and ashen, it fell down my back and framed my face. I smiled into the mirror.

When Van woke up, I heated a can of chicken noodle soup and put it on a tray with saltines. I sat there and watched her eat. When she was finished, Van said, "Thank you."

"You don't have to thank me for anything."

"You're not going to say anything to Mom and Dad, are you?"

"No."

"Or Sef?"

I shook my head. I remembered when Van and I used to lie next to each other and play the Truth Game. "Truth or truth?"

"Truth."

"Do you really think Finn was good for you?"

"Was, as in past tense?"

"Yeah. Remember, it was only for a few months, Van."

"I know, but I can't help it, as in present tense. Those months seemed like forever." She sighed. "But I'm mad. I feel like an idiot. I just wanted him to like me."

She covered her eyes with her hand. "I just did things. I wanted to zone out, you know. I don't even like drinking that much. I just wanted to do whatever Finn did."

"I saw him driving his car one night with someone else," I said. "I should have told you sooner, but I didn't know if I should."

"I know. He has all these 'friends' that are girls. Can't say that helped our relationship too much."

"Yeah, he could have treated you better. Starting that night with Kristen."

"I know you think it's all because of Sef, but it started before Sef left. I don't know, maybe Sef would have straightened me out a long time ago. It's hard to say. But Sef's not perfect. Even if he seems to be sometimes."

"No, he's not perfect," I repeated, letting that sink in.

"And I thought Finn really liked me—you know, like forever. And it was such an escape from everything."

"That's why I run. Just to escape."

"That seems like a slightly healthier outlet."

I laughed. "Your friends must be happy—they'll get to see you again."

"That's true. I miss them. They liked the stories, but they said I was MIA."

"You were definitely missing in action," I said.

"In one of his emails Sef said one thing he'd learned was to live his life like every day was his last, and he'd want to be with people who really liked him and he really liked. It depended what I wanted."

"Sef said that?"

"Yeah, guess he's gotten pretty profound over there." Van smiled. "Truth or truth?"

"Truth."

"Do you think Sef will be all right?"

"Yeah. He has to be."

When Mom and Dad got home, I told them that Van didn't feel well, and I stayed with her the rest of the night until she fell asleep again. I felt closer to Van than I had in a long time. What happened today was our secret. I couldn't do anything for Blue Sky, but I could help Van. And Jack too.

CHAPTER 42

LOOK FOR ME

To: Cassie

From: Blue Sky

Subject: Interview

Dear Cassie,

I answer all your interview questions now for your class.
That is it. We leave. I am to sad.

1. My blog name is Blue Sky because when I think of
Iraq in passed days I think of blue sky spread forever. I start
to write blog because my cousin do. He tell me. Now I write
because writing makes me feel much more good.

2. I am 13 years old. My first memory is of my 3 birthday.
I have photo of the day. My grandfather is there with me. The
cake is chocolate inside and vanilla outside with flowers. I am
happy.

3. My life center around my family and school and friends.
Now we spend most time home and school when safe but

before we travel and I miss that. We try to stay normal but home is like jail because of bombings and raids and war on us. Some days I measure time by number of bombs fall. The sky is terror. Hard to say in words what war do to us.

4. Chocolate cake is my best food.

5. I like to study English. My bad subject is physics. If I study better I figure out how to go to the moon and live.

6. I have one old sister. We share a bedroom and fight much. And one younger brother, 2. He stopped talking after a loud bomb. Now he say some words.

7. My mother is a doctor and my father is English teacher and translator.

8. My dream is to help rebuild Iraq one day. That take my life.

9. I tell the world Iraq was a beautiful place. I love my country. One time it will be beautiful and have peace and blue sky. No war, no bombs.

10. I want my name to be my own name. My Iraqi name not my blog name Blue Sky. I who I was born. I hope for my children to live safe and I wish to live and die in my own country.

Thank you for your words over time. I not miss the heat without running water and electricity or the sound of fighter planes, tanks, dogs crazy barking. May Allah protect us from what is to come. I hope your brother Sef come home quick and safe and this war end. Look for me in the blue sky.

My breath caught in my throat like I was going to choke. I pushed it through. I had to. I opened my window to look up at the sky that had turned dark gray and thick with clouds. I thought I could make out a few stars. They were barely visible, but they were there. I kept looking up at the sky because I wanted to believe in something higher than here on earth.

But I was here. Right here. Soft rain was coming down now, melting the snow. I licked a drop from the windowsill. It was warm and tasted like dirt. All of us were trying to escape from some pain. We each had our own way of dealing with what we were afraid of. I looked up at the sky then and prayed that Blue Sky's family would be safe.

CHAPTER 43

THE LETTING GO

JACK HAD PILED Mom's poetry books up next to the bookshelf. He was flipping through one of them. The phone rang. Mom's head jerked up like it always did when the phone rang. Jack's head snapped back, too. "Sef," he said. "Sef is calling me."

"Oh, my God, Jack! You talked!" Mom yelled. "And it's Sef! Why does everything always happen at once!" Her voice cracked when she snatched up the phone and said, "Hello?"

"Sef!" She fell back on the chair and started to cry. "I know, I know, I'm trying. Are you all right? Thank you for calling."

Jack bolted back and forth in the living room. "It's Sef! It's Sef!"

"Jack, Sef wants to talk to you," Mom said.

Jack clutched on to the phone. For a minute, I thought he wasn't going to say anything. I came closer. I could hear Sef's voice like a murmur, a stream coming from the other side of the world, and everything was good again.

"They're fine," Jack told Sef. "I'm taking care of everyone. But I want to drive a tank. I got my Christmas presents. Now I can come to Iraq with you."

I heard Sef laughing, and my chest hurt. He was so close.

Mom said, "Cass is next."

"My friend Cass is next," Jack said. "How are the troops doing? Okay, ten four." He said good-bye and passed the phone to me.

"Hey, Sef." I turned away from the others.

"Hey, Cass. How are things?"

"Things are okay. I miss you, Sef. Nothing's the same here." I glanced at Mom. "But things are fine. Everyone's fine, really. Except Finn broke up with Van."

"Well, that's good, right? See you later, peaze train!" He laughed. "Are you running?"

"Yeah, I'm running, but not with sixty pounds on my back."

"We'll race when I get home."

"Yeah, when you get home. I can't wait, Sef. I can't wait." My voice echoed back at me as Mom pried the phone out of my hands.

I stood close to the phone to hear his voice talking to Van, Dad, and then Mom again. When Mom hung up, it was suddenly too quiet. Even though all five of us were here, the room felt empty.

Mom wiped her eyes and turned to Jack and said, "You talked, Jack. And you knew Sef was calling. How did you know that? Come here, baby."

"I knew. I was waiting." Jack frowned. "And I'm not a baby. I'm going to Iraq with Sef."

Jack looked at me, his hands clenched. He came closer, crouching a little as he walked, squinting through his thick glasses.

"What is it?" I asked.

"What is a retard?"

We looked at each other. No one said anything. He said it louder, "What is a retard?"

Mom cried out, "You're not a retard. Who said that?"

Jack turned to me, waiting.

I said, "Someone who does things a little slower than other people."

A huge smile spread over Jack's face. "I'm so fast. Look at me." He struck a running pose and sprinted from the living room into the kitchen. He did it again and again, and we laughed.

Mom clapped. "You're the fastest one around here. I missed you. It's been too quiet around here."

He stopped in front of Dad. "I don't want to talk to Ben Adams ever, ever, ever."

Mom looked at Dad.

"If that's what you want, Jack. You're the boss," Dad said.

"Oh, honey." Mom held her face in her hands and cried.

Jack wasn't through. He crossed his arms and faced us. "I'm going to Iraq. I'm going to sign up."

"You're not old enough." Mom tilted her head toward him.

"I need to go," Jack said. "I'm going there, and I'm going to be just like Sef. I'm going to *be* Sef."

"Oh, Jack," Mom said.

"You have to be Jack," I said. "You don't want to be anyone else. And remember you promised Sef you'd take care of everyone while he was gone?"

Jack frowned.

"Besides, you're just right the way you are. I'd miss you if you were Sef."

"Me too," Mom said. "I'd be so lonely. It's bad enough having Sef over there."

Jack took a deep breath. "I'm just right?"

"Yes," I said.

"Jack is?" He breathed out. He seemed to give in to his body.

"Yes, Jack is."

Jack was lying in bed with Mom's book open on his chest. "Can you read this to me?" He flipped the book over.

I did. It was open to a poem called "After Great Pain." I read the last lines. "This is the Hour of Lead/Remembered, if outlived,/As Freezing persons, recollect the Snow—/First—Chill—then Stupor, then the letting go."

Jack said, "Then the letting go," and he closed his eyes. I slid off his cracked glasses.

CHAPTER 44

BREATHE

AFTER SCHOOL JACK was doing push-ups and sit-ups in the kitchen. "I'm gonna be so fast and strong. Feel this."

He flexed one arm, then the other. I squeezed.

"Pretty good, but if you're really going to be fast, you should run."

"Like Sef?"

"Yup. With me. Get your sneaks on."

He stared at me.

"Why not?" I took his hand.

He followed me out in his camouflage and sneakers. The snow was dripping from the trees.

"Like this?" Jack bolted down the sidewalk as fast as he could, kicking up slush behind him.

"Not too fast, or you'll be wiped out right away."

He sprinted, walked, then jogged beside me. I went slowly like Sef did for me when I first started with him. The air felt good on my face, and I liked hearing the *pit pat* of Jack's feet beside mine.

After a loop, we headed back. When our house came in view, Jack said, "You need me here. I have to take care of everyone."

"That's right," I said.

"I have to do everything Sef did."

"Well, maybe not everything, but a lot of things. You might even beat him in a race when he comes back."

Jack beamed. After a minute, he said, "But I didn't kill anyone."

"Who killed someone?" I asked.

"You know. Sef."

"How do you know?"

"He did."

"Well, what do you think happened?"

"He was scared, and it was dark."

I tried to look in Jack's eyes, but he was looking up at the sky. "Did you see him? Have you actually *seen* Sef since he left, Jack?"

He stopped and squinted up at me. The corner of his mouth lifted. "Sometimes."

"Does he say anything?"

"He tells me to 'Breathe! Dammit, breathe. You have to!'"

"Like when you were at the ocean that time?"

He nodded.

"Did you tell Mom that?"

"No."

"Did Sef say anything else to you?"

"No. Don't worry, Cass." He smiled at me.

When we got home, Van was making chocolate chip cookies. "I made it super buttery and with extra chocolate chips."

"It's not your execution meal, is it?" I asked her, smiling as I scraped around the side of the bowl with my finger.

"Not quite." She smiled. "It's Finn's."

I laughed and took a spoonful of the dough. Jack did too.

"What would you have for your last meal if you could have anything, Jack?" Van asked.

"Hot dogs like Dad makes and ice cream. But I want them every day."

"Good plan," I said. "Yum, this is so good. Why would anyone cook this stuff?"

"Um, so they don't get sick?" Van said.

"Don't tell Mom. It's so good."

Spoon after spoon, we ate almost half the bowl before Van said, "Okay, I think I'm officially sick now."

"I'm never sick!" Jack yelled. He took the old umbrella stroller out of the back of the closet. "Can we?"

Van and I looked at each other. "Sure, why not?"

He got in, and we took turns zooming him down the hallway, through the kitchen, and around the corner into the living room like we used to. I looped around so fast, the stroller skidded on two wheels.

"Faster," Jack said. We tied him in with a scarf and went even faster. Laughing, zipping back and forth until Van said, "I need to stop." She lay on the couch. "I think I'm going to die."

"Me too," I said.

"I feel great!" Jack tried to push himself with his feet in the stroller.

"A week until your birthday, Van," I said.

"Sweet sixteen," she said sarcastically. She sighed and wiped the corners of her eyes. "Why is everything so hard sometimes?"

"I can help." Jack put his face close to Van's. "Breathe."

"Breathe?" she said.

He took deep breaths in and out. "Like that."

Van smiled and breathed.

That night Dad came home early. The warm air must have gotten to him. "I'll fire up the grill," he said to Mom.

"There's still snow out there," she said.

"A little snow isn't going to hurt the burgers any."

"Suit yourself." Mom laughed as he headed out armed with his grilling spatulas and tongs.

"Looks like you're going to get your hot dog," Van said to Jack.

It wasn't long before the smoke was rising from the grill in gray slivers. I helped Mom cut tomatoes and lettuce for the salad. Van baked the rest of her cookies, and Jack ran in circles around the kitchen table, punching the air. "I'm going to be faster than Sef!"

When we sat down to eat, Dad raised his Heineken. "Cheers," he said.

"Cheers!" Mom raised her wine, and Jack lifted his glass of milk.

"Listen, I've been thinking that we should go away for the weekend just to relax. Maybe to the Cape to that same place we went before."

Jack jumped up. "Without Sef?"

No one said anything. Dad swallowed his beer.

"Without Sef?" he said again. "I can't swim without Sef."

"It's winter," Van said. "It's too cold to swim."

But Jack never got cold. "You can swim, Jack. You can do everything," I said. I wondered if Jack still felt like he was dying sometimes. Did he lose his breath too and feel his heart pounding like crazy? Is that why Sef told him to breathe?

"He said I could do anything."

"You *can* do anything," I said. "You're the one."

"Yup. I'm so fast, no one can stop me." He ran from one end of the kitchen to the other, stopping at last in front of me. His eyes shone pale blue like mine, but they were blurry behind his glasses. He said, "Here I am."

Later when I went upstairs, I saw that the door to Jack's room was open. Jack was asleep on his bed with White Kitty tucked into his camouflage shirt, her head poking out the neck. He still had on his running sneakers.

I remembered him choking at the beach that day when he was little, as Sef whacked him on the back and told him to breathe, to stay alive. Told him he could do anything. I closed my eyes and forced breath through my body. *Sef was close.* I could see him and hear him. I pushed air in and out. *I could breathe.* We were all in this together.

FRESH REDUX

To: Rob
From: Cassie
Subject: Fresh

   Still wanna go? If yes, when?

                      C

To: Cassie
From: Rob
Subject: Re: Fresh

   2morrow?

        R

The next day when I collected Jack, I didn't tell him we were
going to Fresh. We walked out of school like we always did.
I waved to Rob, who said good-bye to his friends and jogged
over. "Hey, Cass. Jack. Gimme five, man."

"We're going to Fresh, Jack," I said. "You can get whatever you want."

"Let's go!" Jack said, stomping his feet, right then left then right.

"Are we marching there?" Rob asked me.

"Ask the marine," I said.

Rob laughed. His hand brushed mine as we walked behind Jack. "So why'd you wait so long to email me again?" Rob asked quietly.

"I was waiting for you to email me."

"I emailed you last."

"No you didn't."

"Yes I did."

"It's probably sitting in your unsent messages."

Jack turned around. "Are you guys fighting?"

"No," I said. "Rob just has memory loss."

Jack looked from me to Rob and back, then yelled, "Race you!" He sprinted ahead.

We ran the whole way there. Inside smelled of chocolate and butter and fresh bread. At the counter, a blender was whirring and a girl in overalls was steaming milk. We ordered three slices of chocolate pie. It had meringue on the bottom, a layer of chocolate, a layer of chocolate and whipped cream, and whipped cream on the top. Rob wouldn't let me pay. "It was my idea," he said, carrying the tray to our table.

"I asked you," I said.

"Jack, tell your sister to believe me. It's like she barely noticed me for months, and now she's giving me a hard time. I mean, did you ever look at me once?"

"Okay, I'm looking at you now," I said. "You have whipped cream on your chin."

He groaned and wiped it off.

"Can I get another?" Jack asked.

"You'll be sick, Jack."

"No I won't. I never get sick."

"Sure, you can have another," Rob told Jack. He turned to me. "I'm going to ask you the next time. Let's just get that out in the open."

"When?" I asked.

The next morning at school, Sonia was at the bathroom mirror brushing her hair when I went to wash my hands.

She tilted her head and smoothed her bangs. "Your hair looks good down."

"Thanks." I flipped it over my shoulder so it fell down my back.

"You should wear it like that all the time."

I realized this was the first time I'd seen Sonia without anyone else around. Why was I nervous?

"I heard you went to Fresh with Rob," she said.

"Yeah. Jack went too." More quietly, I said, "Is that why you're talking to me now?"

She folded her brush and slipped it in her backpack. "My mom said I should talk to you. She said it wasn't your fault. You know, whatever stupid thing happened between my dad and your mom. I don't even want to think about it."

She smiled a little. I did too.

I tried to remember all the things that I wanted to tell her. "I feel like you snapped on me because I don't know why—I'm not perfect or cool enough or something." I shook the water from my hands. "I mean, okay, we are kind of crazy, but at least we realize that, and we're trying to make things better. And it wasn't really anything to do with me anyway—what happened."

She turned to me as if she was going to say something else. But the bathroom door opened and someone came in along with the hallway noise of students on their way to their next classes, and then the moment was gone.

Toward the end of lunch, Rob came over and sat with me and Kim. I saw Sonia watching us.

"Hope I'm not interrupting," he said.

"Kim was just telling me that her cousin is coming home from Iraq," I said.

"Sef is next," Kim said.

"Tell me that again," I said.

She did.

"You know everything is okay, right?" Rob said.

"Not really. Why would I?" I asked.

"Because it is. Right now it is." He shrugged. "My mom's a Buddhist."

I stared at him. "Oh, yeah?"

He smiled. "Her favorite saying is 'You only lose what you cling to.'"

I put down my sandwich. "How do you stop clinging?"

"You breathe in. And out." He breathed dramatically. "And let it go. You try, anyway."

I did. I breathed in and out. "There's going to be a lot of breathing going on," I said.

"Yup," Rob said. "A little deeper."

"Like this?" I said.

"Maybe not so loud," Rob told me.

Kim cracked up. "Somehow I don't think this is what your mom had in mind."

We were all breathing so hard at once, we started laughing until we were choking.

GHOSTS

To: Cassie

From: Sef

Subject: Baghdad school

Hi Cass,

Today we went to this girls' school close to where we're stationed because we're supposed to be making connections here. I saw a girl who reminded me of you. She had her hair pulled back like yours, and she was about your age. I asked her what we could do to help. At first she didn't say anything. Neither did her friends. They were too polite or something. I asked again. She finally said, "You could go back to your country."

She wasn't trying to be mean or anything, really. She just really wanted us to leave. The truth is I'm just trying to stay alive—to keep all of us alive. I didn't tell you, but Mark was injured pretty badly. He's in a hospital in Germany now. A couple others too. And one of the guys in another troop was found dead in the showers. I met him before. He seemed like everyone else. He was married, and his wife was pregnant. They're saying it was an electrical problem, as in cover-up for a suicide. There's no way. I know I shouldn't tell you any of this, but I feel like you want to know what's going on. I've heard it's happening at home too. Scary to think these could be your own guys. Now I have a whole new set of nightmares.

We had to raid a house the other night. We were told they were terrorists, but I can't tell who's a terrorist and who's not. We just do what we're told. Someone emptied a sack of flour all over the kitchen. The family was still in their pajamas. There were these white footprints everywhere, like ghosts were walking around. The women were crying, and all I could think of was Mom. What if it were Mom? When we left, we gave the kids chocolate bars.

I get this big feeling that I should pray, but I don't know how to. My goal is to learn. It's starting to get hot already. Supposed to be 120 in July. Jason would melt. I'm going to stop now. Give me a good kick in the butt—I'm complaining like a baby.

Don't tell Mom yet, but we might have our tour extended. I have to keep these guys safe. They are doing that much for me.

Stay strong for me. Miss you.

Love,

Sef

To: Blue Sky
From: Cassie
Subject: No Subject

Dear Blue Sky,

Thank you for writing and answering my questions. I hope
you and your family are safe, no matter what happens. I wish
I knew where you were. Looks like Sef's tour will probably
be extended. I miss hearing from you. Jack started talking
again. I hope your brother is still talking. Tomorrow I present
you to my social studies class. I won't forget you, Blue Sky.
Ever. I will think of you every day. Write to me when you can.
I'll be waiting.

Cassie

THE THING
WITH FEATHERS

IN SOCIAL STUDIES the next day, I stood before the class. Mr. Barkan was at his desk with his head down, chewing on his glasses. He had the same too-short brown pants he always wore and his clunky shoes. I pressed my paper as tightly as I could. The words blurred on the page. I thought of Blue Sky and tried to keep my voice steady as I read her interview questions.

When I finished, I looked at Rob and took a deep breath. He smiled at me. Mr. Barkan asked, "Do you want to tell us why you chose Blue Sky?"

"I chose her because she lives in Iraq, and that's where my brother is fighting. And because of a song Sef used to listen to called 'Good-bye Blue Sky.' "

Kim looked up from her doodling and grinned. I hadn't told her that part. Someone thumped his hands on his desk.

"No musical interludes necessary," Mr. Barkan said. "Thank you, Cassie. Who has a question?"

I looked around the room.

"Does Blue Sky *want* to go to school?" Lisa asked.

"Yes, believe it or not. But it was too dangerous getting there with all the bombs going off and people disappearing. So a lot of days, she couldn't get there even if—"

"Like a snow day, but a bomb day." Brandon smiled and his eyes darted around the room. "I'd love to miss a couple of days because of *bombs*."

A few people laughed.

"Bombs are a little different than snow," I said. "Besides, she can't even leave her house, and they often have no electricity or running water."

Dave Swanson said, "Cool."

"That is totally not cool," Michaela said.

"Can you tell us a little about what you think of the war in general?" Mr. Barkan asked.

"I'm against the war, but I support Sef," I admitted. "I actually didn't think about the war that much before Sef went there, and I didn't think about their side of it at all until I read Blue Sky's blog."

Mr. Barkan stood and walked in front of the class. "Do you see what a difference it makes to read another person's point of view? You get a more complete understanding of history by seeing both sides. How's your brother doing over there?"

"He's doing all right, but he says everything's a mess. He sees people die, cars and buildings blown up every day." I glanced at Sonia. She was the only one who actually knew him.

Dave sat forward in his chair. His eyes were bright. "It must be like A & A, this awesome video game I play."

241

"It's real," I said. "It's not a video game."

"A & A is totally real. I can be any general and blow up—"

"Now are you going to ask her how many people her brother has blown away?" Brandon asked.

"Okay. How many people has your brother blown away?" Dave asked.

I wasn't going to tell them anything. They didn't know a thing about Sef. Everything looked grainy, like rain on glass in front of me. I started shaking. I couldn't breathe. My paper slipped between my fingers. I looked at Rob and remembered what he'd said to me before. "You only lose what you cling to."

"Cassie, are you all right?" Mr. Barkan asked.

I couldn't feel myself. I ran out the door, down the hallway, and through the front entrance of the school into the cold air. I kept going all the way down to the football field, to the bleachers. I sat on the bleachers and put my head between my knees. Underneath the metal seats, there was a dead bird on the top of the snow. Little and brown and speckled—a sparrow, I guessed. I thought of what Blue Sky had written on her blog. "Hope is the thing with feathers." My face was wet and cold. I shivered and wiped under my eyes with my sweatshirt. Sef wasn't going to die. He couldn't. I should have said that instead of running away. I would. I swore it.

Someone was walking out to get me. Sonia. She stood in front of me.

"Did Mr. Barkan send you to get me?"

She nodded.

"I just couldn't breathe in there. I have to work on my breathing." I laughed a little.

She nodded. "Can I sit down?"

"Yeah."

"I've been acting like a jerk. I shouldn't have blamed you for my dad. It wasn't fair." She kicked the ice with her brown leather riding boots. "I just didn't want to believe he would act like that with my best friend's mother. I didn't want to believe it at all. I'm sorry."

"I'm sorry, too. I'm sorry things got so messed up. Everything got so stressful with Sef."

"No." She shook her head. "Please don't apologize for Sef."

I pointed to the dead sparrow.

"Don't look at that. He's going to come home again, Cassie, and he's going to be fine."

"You don't know if he'll be fine." I turned to her. "He's never going to be the same again. He won't be the Sef who left. Do you know what that means?"

She looked down, and I could tell that I had hurt her.

"He'll still be Sef," she said softly, and pulled her sweater tighter around her. "Hey, let's bury this bird after school. I'll get a box."

"Okay," I said. I saw *her*—not the clothes, the hair, the make-up—just Sonia.

"We should go back. It's freezing out here."

"Mr. Barkan is going to think we took off," I said.

"Maybe we should," she said. "Remember when we were going to run away to Swallow River?"

"Yeah, nobody would have ever found us there," I joked.

We started back across the frozen field.

"Thanks for getting me," I said.

"Anything to get out of social studies." She smiled at me. "So are you going to tell me about Rob, or what?"

"I like him."

"No kidding." She laughed.

"And I think he likes me. I mean just for me."

"Just for you." She looked at me then as if she was seeing me—Cassie—for the first time in a long time. "You can sit with us at lunch if you want."

I said, "You can sit with us too."

CHAPTER 48

EVERY LAST THING

WE TOOK FRIDAY off of school to go to the Cape. It was a little rainy but mild, and I could smell the sea. I felt for my blue stone in my pocket. We carried our things into the hotel and unpacked. Then Van, Jack, and I headed for the beach.

"When I grow up, I'm going to go to the Dolphin Inn whenever I want," Jack said. "Every week."

"I guess you're going to be rich," Van said.

"I'm going to be Jack," he said. "Just Jack."

Van smiled. "I'm glad you're talking again, Jack."

"Me too. I can do anything—right, Cass? I'm never ever going to die!" Jack ran ahead, kicking the sand.

"Truth or truth?" I asked Van.

"Truth."

She looked up at the sun, her eyes brownish hazel in the light. She wore sneakers and jeans like me, and a black sweater, which along with her dark hair made her face paler, even more striking.

"What do you want to be?" I asked.

"I don't want to be afraid of everything."

"You can be Supergirl, too!" Jack shouted into the wind.

"*You're* Supergirl?" Van smiled at me.

"Yup."

"Truth or truth, Supergirl?" Van asked.

"Truth."

"What do you want to be?"

"I want Sef to come home."

"Me too, but what do you want for you? Just you."

"To be happy." I thought of what Blue Sky had said. *No one is happy about a thing until it is lost.* I wanted to be happy before anything was lost. Right now.

I breathed in the salty air. I said, "I had a dream about Blue Sky. She said that I wouldn't remember her. I told her that I would. I couldn't see her anywhere. I could just hear her talking. I told her that I'd remember every last thing. But I don't know if she heard me. There was just cloudy air all around me." I pointed up. "Like this."

"Blue Sky didn't disappear. And I bet she wouldn't want you to worry about her," Van said.

"It's just weird that no one here seems to care much," I said.

"Yeah, it's a lot easier when you don't have to think about war and people dying and stuff."

"But we have to think about it, Van. We have to—to make things better," I said. "Like Sef would."

"Yeah," Van said. "But it's hard."

Seagulls screamed past us.

"Things okay on the Finn front?" I asked.

"Finn who?" she said.

"Finn peaze train!" Jack yelled.

"Does he hear everything?" Van asked.

"I think so. He knows that Sef killed someone," I whispered. "Don't ask how. He just does. He knows way more than I ever knew."

Jack bolted over the wet sand, skipping over the breaking waves. I'd always thought about how he needed us, but we needed him just as much. Maybe even more.

Jack lay down and spread out his arms and legs in the sand, making an angel. "And miles to go before I sleep," he said softly. "And miles to go before I sleep."

"Van?" I asked.

"Yeah?"

"Do you remember when we used to go sledding?"

"I remember being scared to death." She laughed. "I was always scared, and you were always in the front. And we'd go so fast."

"I was scared too. I just pretended not to be," I said.

"Do you remember 'You will fly to success!'?" I asked her.

"Sef's fortune cookie?"

I nodded. "Do you believe in those things?"

"Yeah, I guess. You've got to believe in something."

"Yeah, that's true," I said. "We have to believe that no matter what happens, we'll be okay. Swear on it, Van. Swear you'll be here for me when I need you. Swear that you won't disappear again."

"I swear."

"I do too."

I looked up. The winter sun was barely visible in the haze. I said, "Doesn't it seem like he's been gone for a long time?"

"So long. About a lifetime."

"I didn't think we'd be able to do it. To" —I paused—"I don't know, *live* without him. But we are. We are living." I laughed and the wind carried my laughter.

Jack got up and sprinted toward the water. Van held my arm when I started after him. "Wait," she said.

He ran straight in, his arms flapping above the waves, until he was waist-high. "Sef! Sef!" he yelled. "Look at me. I can swim! I can do anything!" He whooped it up, then charged back to shore. "It's too cold. I'll swim more later."

I looked to the golden eye of the sun as I ran across the sand toward the water. A wave crashed, and the sea sprayed up on my face and arms. This was my life.

"Come on!" I called to Jack and Van, and I took off running down the beach, breathing.

ACKNOWLEDGMENTS

I am forever grateful to my agent, Lane Zachary, my editor, Nancy Paulsen, and associate editor Sara Kreger.

To all the Iraqi girl bloggers brave enough to write about how the war changed their lives.

To the soldiers who fought in the war, and the families they left behind.

To Marcia and Harry Garvey for giving me a place to write, and to Hoodie for every Tuesday.

And to Chris, Tess, Calla, CC, and Malcolm—for everything else.